MW00522853

The Ghosts of Castle Pinckney
A Charlestonian's true tales of his boyhood
on a harbor island

by

E. P. McClellan, Jr.

Illustrated by Bill Smith

With a brief history by Suzannah Smith Miles

"In a Castle Dark or a Fortress Strong, with Chains Upon My Feet" – Gordon Lightfoot

Main entrance (sally port) to Castle Pinckney. Photo by Bill Smith.

Narwhal Press Inc.
Charleston/Miami

FIRST EDITION

Copyright © 1998 by E. P. McClellan, Jr.

Library of Congress Catalog Card Number: 98-065031

ISBN: 1-886391-18-1 (hard cover)
ISBN: 1-886391-19-x (paperback)

Front cover: (clockwise) photos of the author, the author's boyhood home, the Castle Pinckney kids (circa 1928-1935), aerial view of Castle Pinckney (circa 1960), unidentified man in front of the walls of Castle Pinckney (Civil War era).

Back cover: 1998 photo of the author, and letters by SiAra Washington, Jamaine Venning, Shalita, and Laura Marie Julich.

All rights reserved, including the right to reproduce this publication or portions in any form, except for brief quotations in a review.

All correspondence and inquiries should be directed to the publisher, Narwhal Press Inc., 1629 Meeting Street, Charleston, SC 29405.

Printed in the United States of America.

Dedication

This book is respectfully dedicated:

To Susan, my bride of fifty-plus years.

To our sons Chris, Barry and Brian and our special daughters-in-law.

To our exciting grandchildren who, through the course of twenty years, filled my heart with warmth as they listened intently to my stories:

Melanie Jane McClellan
Kelley Jean McClellan
Jacob Ezra McClellan
Joshua Aaron McClellan

Orion Palmer McClellan
Robert Edward McClellan
Matthew George McClellan
Rachel Elizabeth McClellan

To the teachers and exuberant "second graders" at Mamie P. Whitesides Elementary School, Mt. Pleasant, South Carolina, who humbled me with their gratitude and letters each time I visited to tell my stories. (I consider their letters to me to be among my most precious possessions.)

Acknowledgments

I would also like to acknowledge the help given to me by:

Brenda Godfrey who, early on, helped immeasurably with the manuscript.

Maggie Myatt, the little "Fireball," who exercised her computer skills to finalize the manuscript and stimulated the pursuit of publication.

Dr. E. Lee Spence for the conceptualization and design of my book, including the contribution of many of the historical illustrations.

Bill Smith, for his wonderful drawings of my childhood memories.

The staff of Fort Moultrie, the U.S. National Park Service, Special Collections–College of Charleston, Narwhal Press Inc., and *The Post and Courier.*

– E. P. McClellan, Jr.

PREFACE

Centrally located in Charleston Harbor is a small island with an impressive, but now crumbling, brick fort, slowly succumbing to the ravages of storms, tides and time.

The island is Shutes Folly. Folly refers not to any lack of judgment on the part of the original owner, but describes the lush vegetation once found on the island. Some might incorrectly think the name better describes the fort, as the word "folly" can also mean "a whimsical or extravagant and often useless structure." The fortification is correctly called Castle Pinckney and sits within sight of a much more famous island structure, Fort Sumter. The castle, built in the early 1800s on the site of a Revolutionary War fort, was named in honor of General Charles Cotesworth Pinckney.

During the Civil War, the old brick fortress had been filled with earth to within three or four feet of the top perimeter. Within the walls of the fortress, the U.S. Corps of Engineers had erected a one-and-a-half-story, four-bedroom residence, a small office building, and a large warehouse. In the warehouse, supplies and equipment were stored for use by the Corps. On the southern side of the house and angling in front of the warehouse was a substantial dock extending some three hundred feet into the harbor.

For a while, the island's only inhabitant was a night watchman. He was quartered in the office building. It is doubtful that he knew much, if anything at all, about the island's history. The island had played a much-ignored secondary role in both the Revolutionary War and the Civil War. Perhaps it is best described as more of a legend than a prominence in history. However, the island is no mere legend to me and my family, and this book tells of a six-year period when the fort came to life with children who walked among the ghosts of the fort during the Great Depression.

This came about because, in the summer of 1928, my father became an inspector for the Corps. Uprooting the family from McClellanville, South Carolina, he moved us into 87 Smith Street on the Charleston peninsula.

From his new office at the Customs House on East Bay Street, my father had a good view of Castle Pinckney. Deciding that it would be a wonderful and unique place to live, he inquired about the unoccupied house and obtained permission to move there.

Shortly after school let out for the summer of 1929, my father, mother, two sisters and I relocated to the middle of Charleston harbor. At the time of the move, I was seven (born April 2, 1922). One sister was two and a half years my senior, the other was three and a half years my junior.

We were considered to be in the Craft School district, and the edifice at "Legare and Queen" became the landmark of my elementary education. Getting to school meant a short boat ride to the "Engineer dock" at Charleston and a good walk.

I explored every conceivable route to school. I learned all the streets in that area of the old city and, by changing routes to and from school, I became thoroughly acquainted with almost all of its homes, businesses and landmarks. I cherish the memories of those treks through the "old market" with its maze of shops and stalls, the venders hawking fresh vegetables, meat and fish. I remember the pleasant tones of their voices as they spoke "Gullah," which I later learned was a blend of African and old English.

In the fall of 1934, I got my first bicycle – for transportation – and attended Charleston High School. The following spring, we left our castle home and moved to "Saint Andrews Parish," west of the Ashley.

That was sixty-three years ago, but the memories of the preceding six years, when we lived "proximal to heaven," have not dimmed. This book is my attempt to share those memories.

– E. P. McClellan, Jr.

TABLE OF CONTENTS

Dedication & Acknowledgments iii

Forward...iv

Cranking the Pump 1

Cat in the Cistern 3

Brownie 5

"The Bridge Lighted Up!"...7

Uncle George 9

"Doormat" Flounder 13

The Dummy Line 15

Shark in the Slough 19

A "Gigged" Foot 21

A "Bricken" Neck 25

Nine Little Rats 27

A Big Sheepshead..31

A Fish for Sunday Dinner 35

A Fall from the Dock...39

A Taste of Raisin Wine 43

"My" Creek 47

A Baby Diamondback Terrapin...51

The Day I Found the "IF" 53

To Tell the Truth...57

Rats! 59

Spirits-Bread-Didyap 61

A Sad Sea Voyage 65

Launching the Newly Painted Bateau 71

"Tall Betsy" 75

A Bald Eagle's Perch 79

Fireworks..83

Rattlesnake! 87

A Brief History of Castle Pinckney by Suzannah Smith Miles 101

Return to Castle Pinckney 103

CRANKING THE PUMP

Our primary source of water was rainfall. Gutters on the eaves of the house captured the water and channeled it into a large concrete cistern under the house.

At the back of the house, there was a rectangular tank elevated about ten feet off the ground. From this tank, water flowed by gravity, through the pipes to the kitchen and bathroom.

On the right front side of the house, near the cistern, was a large, heavy-duty pump driven by a very big gasoline engine. This unit was responsible for getting water from the cistern to the tank.

The engine was started by opening a valve in the gas line, priming with a plunger mechanism, setting the throttle, then hand cranking it. It was usually operated by men of the working crew and cranked up as frequently as necessary to keep water available in the tank.

I always had a measure of curiosity about that engine and pump. I would watch every detail as the men ran through the procedure of getting it going.

Often, after the work crew had gone for the day, I would attempt to start the engine myself. I was just not strong enough to turn the engine over with the heavy hand-crank.

On one occasion, we were expecting relatives and friends to visit for the weekend. My mother became exceedingly alarmed when she turned on the spigot in the kitchen and there was no water.

The work crew had gone for the weekend and my father was not expected home any time soon.

I thought to myself, "I'm ten now and I should be man enough to crank that engine!" So, armed with some degree of determination, off I went to give it a try.

Again, I went through the starting procedure, as I had done so many times without reward. I made sure everything was in proper order. Intently, I grabbed the crank handle and tried to give it a whirl. It would not budge. I felt so frustrated. We needed water and my mother's anxiety already had reached the level of distress. I was the only one who could help.

I latched onto the crank handle with both hands and began to pull up on it. It moved slightly. I was ecstatic! My determination to crank that engine zoomed to "ten" on a scale of "one to ten." Again, I gripped the crank handle. I said to my arm, "Muscle, do your stuff." With every ounce of strength I could muster, I applied the power. It worked! I cranked the engine! "Pop, pop... pop," it began, then moved into the usual rhythm of normal operation. I adjusted the throttle and listened to the "music."

My mother heard the noise and came running from the kitchen out onto the porch to see what happened. "Did you start that engine?" she screamed over the whine of the motor. I yelled, "Yes, Ma'am, I shore did! Me and my muscle!"

Mama was so happy and so relieved. She hugged me and made me feel proud of my accomplishment.

I let the pump run until the overflow pipe on the tank began to spill water. Then, I cut it off, just like the workmen did.

I had reached a milestone. I had mastered a long-standing challenge, me and my muscle!

CAT IN THE CISTERN

Periodically, the cistern containing our water supply was pumped out, cleaned, and readied for a fresh supply of rain.

Castle Pinckney was a haven for cats. Children like pets and cats are cute, soft and cuddly. Cats get big and then there are more cats. As time goes by, there are more and more cats.

Once, my mother said to my father, "Please arrange to dispose of some of these cats. We now have twenty-eight and there soon will be more!"

The cat thing had reached alarming proportions. Everyone was talking about, worrying about, and predicting all manner of grief for the cats. My father, becoming exceedingly aware of the predicament, decided the time had come to dispatch the cats.

He had threatened many times to do just that, but couldn't seem to muster the courage, or whatever it takes, to get rid of cats.

The day for cistern-cleaning came. The workmen lifted the heavy iron manhole cover off the access. They placed a large hose down in the cistern and began the task of pumping out and cleaning the cistern.

It was necessary for us to store a supply of water because there would be none available while the cistern was being cleaned. Even then, we'd have to wait until the next rainfall. It only took a day to finish the cleaning, but the rain depended on "you know who!"

After draining and cleaning the cistern, the crew chief approached my mother and asked, "How do you suppose that dead cat got in the cistern?" Well, my mother was aghast! "A dead cat in the cistern! Oh dear," she exclaimed, "we've been drinking the water! Oh, my Lord!"

The chief quickly relieved her distress by telling her he was only joking, that there was really no way a cat could get in the cistern. "But, with all the cats around here, I doubt you would miss one or two," he said.

That hint was not lost on my father. He immediately pressed into action. Without going into all the gory details of dispatch, let's just say it was the biggest "Cat-astrophy" in my recollection of life at Castle Pinckney.

We soon learned that the
porch was an ideal skating rink....
Brownie didn't skate, but we would take
turns grabbing her by the tail and she
would run around the porch,
pulling us along.

BROWNIE

Not long after we moved to Castle Pinckney, someone gave us a female German shepherd. We named her Brownie and quickly learned how close a dog can get to your heart. Brownie immediately became one of the family and endeared herself to everyone.

The porch of our house was about ten feet wide and went all around the main part of the house. On the back, it separated the kitchen, dining area and bathroom from the rest of the house. The flooring lumber was tongue and groove oak.

We soon learned that the porch was an ideal skating rink and we spent much time using it for that purpose. Brownie didn't skate, but we would take turns grabbing her by the tail and she would run around the porch, pulling us along. It was so much fun skating, and the rink was complete with banisters for safety. Often, we would come around a corner too fast and be saved by the banister.

We had to be very careful at points of ingress and egress, but, amazingly, no one ever got hurt skating on our rink.

I think Brownie was best at playing hide and seek. We children would hide from her and yell, "Come find me!" She would always find us, no matter how well we hid. It was a long time before we really understood how she could be so good at hide and seek.

Through the marsh area to the right, in front of the house looking toward the big bridge, ran a winding little creek about twelve to fourteen feet wide. It was a Mecca for crabs and I spent many hours there "bringing in the blues."

Most of the time, Brownie would accompany me. At times, when I went alone, I would think about her and whistle. It would not be very long before I could hear her chunking up the creek. Soon, she would be in sight, coming around the bend, swimming toward the bateau.

I'd pull her in and she would express her appreciation by shaking vigorously and giving me a shower.

During those years, I was a self-styled Robinson Crusoe and Brownie was "my man Friday." She was always with me or near by. She followed me everywhere I went. We explored the marsh area and the shoreline together. We didn't exactly eat together, but she was always at the table.

What a wonderful life! What a wonderful companion! We slept in the double bed in the back bedroom. She stretched out on her side of the bed and I on mine. I never told her that she snored!

That night at dusk, as I was looking from the front porch toward the bridge, suddenly, the lights came on. "The bridge lighted up!" I yelled at the top of my voice…. What a magnificent sight. What a beautiful decoration for Charleston's impressive harbor.

"THE BRIDGE LIGHTED UP!"

While we were living on Castle Pinckney, construction of the Grace Memorial Bridge was ongoing. The progress was very slow and one could not detect any day-by-day extension from our vantage point. As time passed, however, the Charleston side and the Mount Pleasant side visibly began to get closer to each other.

Every day, we watched as the men and equipment labored hard and long toward completion. At first, all we could detect was activity on each shore. As time passed, the inclines began to take shape, then the giant spans began to loom. The spans got higher and higher, until they seemed to reach for the sky.

To us, it was like an artist painting a life-sized picture of a prominent landmark. With each phase of construction, the painting became more complete, and more spectacular.

Then came the day when all components of that stately, imposing structure were united in completion. We all but came unglued when the first, tiny little objects began crawling across the giant enhancement to travel.

That night at dusk, as I was looking from the front porch toward the bridge, suddenly, the lights came on. "The bridge lighted up!" I yelled at the top of my voice. I ran all the way to the kitchen where the family had gathered for supper. "The bridge lighted up, the bridge lighted up!"

Everyone scrambled to the porch to take a look. What a magnificent sight. What a beautiful decoration for Charleston's impressive harbor.

It was a spectacular, dramatic conclusion to years of anxiety and suspense. I doubt anyone had a more perfect box seat than ours.

Each night thereafter, until we moved from the island, the game among us kids was to see who would be the first to notice when the lights came on and yell, "The bridge lighted up!"

View of the Old Cooper River Bridge from the "front yard" of Castle Pinckney, circa 1935. Photo courtesy of U.S. National Park Service.

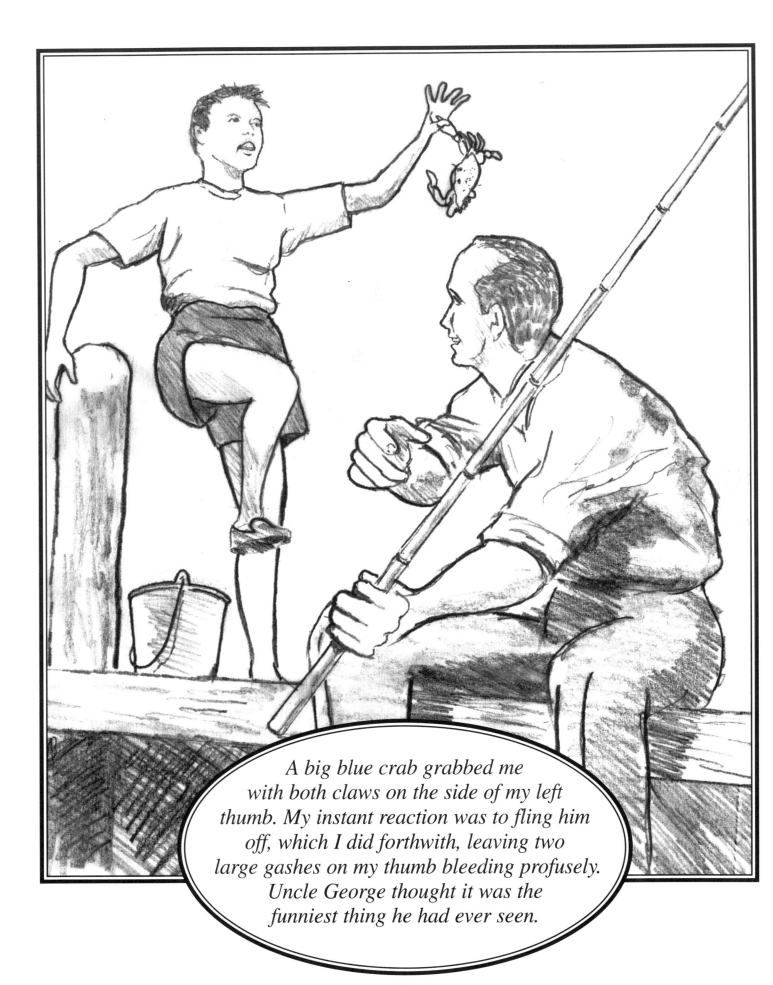

A big blue crab grabbed me with both claws on the side of my left thumb. My instant reaction was to fling him off, which I did forthwith, leaving two large gashes on my thumb bleeding profusely. Uncle George thought it was the funniest thing he had ever seen.

UNCLE GEORGE

My mother's sister lived in Savannah, Georgia, with her husband George and their three children. They were frequent visitors to Castle Pinckney and we, in turn, visited them in Savannah.

Uncle George became ill with a heart attack. His physician suggested that, if possible, he should go somewhere to a place of peace and quiet while recuperating.

Castle Pinckney was just such a place, so Uncle George came to live with us during his convalescence. He was a fine man but not well, not very strong, and somewhat irritable, which is understandable among people with maladies such as his.

He enjoyed his days at Castle Pinckney and spent a great deal of his time fishing from the dock. I tried to be as helpful as I could, since my parents had explained his condition to me. Of course, I didn't really understand the gravity of the circumstances.

I was very mischievous and it seemed like everything I did got on his nerves. Uncle George became more and more intolerant of my capers and antics. On occasion, he would even threaten me with bodily harm. He said he would "break my neck!"

As time went by, I developed a fear of him, although he never struck me or threw anything at me.

He fished for channel bass, using crabs for bait. I would catch crabs for him, pull their backs off, break them in half and put them on his hooks. He was an ardent, successful fisherman. He really caught his share of "spot-tails."

On one occasion, I was attempting to get a crab from the bucket to prepare for baiting his hooks. A big blue crab grabbed me with both claws on the side of my left thumb. My instant reaction was to fling him off, which I did forthwith, leaving two large gashes on my thumb bleeding profusely.

Uncle George thought it was the funniest thing he had ever seen. He just guffawed! I, of course, didn't think it was at all funny and told him to get somebody else to bait his hooks. I went scurrying up the dock to the house to get Mama's help to stop the bleeding and bandage my hand.

It still wasn't funny when Uncle George later related the details, with intermittent laughter, to my parents and sisters. He also enjoyed telling the story to everyone that came to visit.

As time went by, he seemed to feel better and grow stronger. However, one evening at dusk, he came in from the back yard where he had been napping in the hammock. He told my mother he felt rather strange and that everything had gotten dark when he got up.

My mother, perplexed by his symptoms, had no way of knowing or understanding what his problem was. She said to him, "Supper is ready, let's eat, and then we'll go sit on the front porch for a while."

We ate supper, then Mama and Uncle George went to the front porch to sit and talk. My sisters and I stayed in the kitchen to clean up, wash and dry the dishes,

bicker and "cut up," as was customary with the chores.

We were still at it when my mother called us to the front porch. She said, "Uncle George and I were talking and he said, 'Everything is getting dark again,' gasped and slumped in his chair."

On the end of the porch was a bed used to accommodate overflow guests. My mother said, "I need you children to help me slide the chair to the bed and lay him down." I remember her closing his eyelids and putting a nickel on each one.

Mama then began making necessary phone calls to arrange for a boat to come take his body to the funeral home in Charleston. She notified her sister in Savannah and other relatives and friends.

The launch arrived about two o'clock in the morning. The body was put on board by the men who came to help. Uncle George was leaving Castle Pinckney for the last time. It had been a long and quiet night. I remember thinking, "Maybe that crab bite wasn't really all that bad."

My older sister had a thing for ghost stories and frequently told tales to frighten me and our younger sister. One evening, several months after Uncle George's death, as we were finishing supper, my mother told me to go to the front porch and get the "flit gun."

The flit gun was the means we employed to harass mosquitoes, gnats and other insects that seemed to be everywhere all the time. I got up from the table and walked from the kitchen, through the hall, to the front porch. The porch went all the way around the house.

In the afternoon, we children had been playing on the side porch. We left an old wooden high-back bench across the porch, not thinking it would later become a hazard to navigation.

Now, it was very dark and I was on a mission to get the flit gun. It was resting on the floor beside the chair in which Uncle George died. Just as I reached down to pick it up, my older sister yelled out from the kitchen, "You better watch out, too, Uncle George will get you!"

I gasped and gave the flit gun a fling. Instead of going directly back to the kitchen through the hall, I took off like gang-busters around the porch, in the dark, not thinking about that bench. Well, I hit it going full speed. The back of the bench caught me about hip-high and I cut a flip. I must have landed on my feet, because I don't remember losing stride or getting up. I was just running for dear life, and by this time was convinced the ghost of Uncle George had got me!

A split second later, I was in the kitchen, breathless and in tears, wanting to strangle my sister. Everyone was laughing except me. I was really scared, almost broke my neck, and didn't think it was very funny.

I will always remember Uncle George and those two occasions I didn't think were very funny.

"DOORMAT" FLOUNDER

My father was an ardent fisherman. His real thing was "gigging" flounders. Another term the old-timers used was "graining," or "striking."

Gigging or graining or striking, whichever one prefers, employs the same method and equipment: a spear (gig) for the fish, and a light to see them with.

My daddy used a hand-held spotlight connected to an automobile battery. This provided the light to see the fish and the flexibility to shine the light where he wanted it. His fish-catcher was a five-pronged fish spear on the end of a pole about seven feet long.

He would maneuver the bateau through shallow water using the gig as a means of propulsion while shining the light around to spot the fish. They were easy to see as they lay on the bottom, covered with sand or mud. You could see the perfect outline of the fish and two prominent eyes exposed.

His prowess was the envy of all who knew him. He would go gigging anytime the tide and weather were favorable. Whether it was dusk or four a.m., he always seemed anxious to try his luck.

Often, he would invite a friend to spend the night and go gigging. We always had visitors in our home and most of the time there was an abundance of fish to share. Fish not immediately consumed or shared went into the huge brine barrel. We didn't know what refrigeration was back then.

Also, my father was prone to have a little "nip" now and then, or frequently, depending on your take. One night, when a friend came home with him to go gigging, they decided they would take a drink each time they gigged a flounder. They staggered in from the creek after they had gigged number thirteen and my father had fallen out of the boat.

He often took me with him. I sat in the stern of the bateau and watched him as he gigged. My chore was to keep count of the fish. I also had a little four-pronged frog spear, which was just my size. He would often stop the boat, call me to the bow and let me gig a little flounder or maybe a "sailor's choice." I enjoyed getting to use my gig.

One night, he had gigged several flounders of average size. I sat in the stern enjoying the excitement when my father exclaimed, "Here's the old man of the sea!" He drove the gig into the fish and said, "Bring me your little gig. I need to gig him in the tail to stop the fluttering." I moved forward and he planted my little gig into the broad tail of the fish. He told me, "Hold it down as hard as you can." He then jumped overboard to ensure the catch. He placed his free hand under the fish's head where his gig had penetrated. Then, raising the enormous fish from the water, he lifted him over the side of the bateau. It was a memorable moment – he in the water and I in the boat, each of us holding a gig stuck in opposite ends of the big flounder.

Once the fish was safely in the boat, we didn't waste any time going in. We couldn't wait to see that fish on dry land.

In all our years at Castle Pinckney, no one recalls ever having caught a larger flounder. Someone commented, "It looks like a doormat!" It weighed eleven pounds, seven ounces, and just think… my little gig held down the tail!

When I began to apply the brake, the two-by-four broke in two! All the glee abruptly turned to silence, but only for a split second, because at this juncture it appeared as if we were going to roll off the end of the dock.... I quickly sat down and put my foot against the stub.

THE DUMMY LINE

An old brick warehouse, where the Corps of Engineers kept a variety of supplies and equipment, was situated on the main part of the island next to the house. It was a sizable structure and served as headquarters for the work crew.

Between the house and the warehouse, extending down the incline onto the dock and all the way to the loading ramp at the end, was a set of railroad tracks.

On the tracks was a flatbed car with a surface area of about thirty-five square feet. It was maybe five feet wide and seven feet long. This little car was the means of transporting supplies to and from the loading ramp.

It had two axles and four flanged, train-type wheels. Over the right front wheel was a cut-out, for braking purposes. A three-foot section of a two-by-four served as the brake. When placed in the cut-out and pushed against the wheel, the friction would slow the car to a stop.

Its means of propulsion was manpower. When fully loaded, it required four to six workmen to push it, especially up the incline from the dock to the warehouse.

It was fascinating to watch the workmen load the car with supplies from the boat and push it from the end of the dock and up to the warehouse. Sometimes, it would stall on the incline. The men would let it roll slowly back to the level part of the dock. Then, starting over and exerting more effort, they would make sure there was enough power to get it up the incline.

We children affectionately called the system the "Dummy Line." During non-working hours, such as late afternoons and weekends, we spent many happy hours playing on the Dummy Line.

We would roll the car back and forth on the level track between the house and the warehouse. We would take turns riding and pushing, being very careful to keep it safely away from the incline.

There were always children at Castle Pinckney. My two sisters and I were permanent residents, but there were always cousins and friends to add to the count.

We soon learned that, when there were enough of us, we could negotiate the incline with the unloaded car. From then on, the Dummy Line was the central attraction and provided first-class entertainment.

A particular occasion that stands out rather vividly in my mind took place on a weekend when my aunt and her family were visiting.

She had five daughters, and some of them, with several of our friends, together with three of us made for a bunch of youngsters. We converged on the Dummy Line. We would pile on, ride down the incline, picking up a head of steam, and roll to the end of the dock. Then we would all push the car back up to the warehouse area and repeat the adventure. What fun it was!

I was the brake man. The tracks ended abruptly near the end of the dock where the loading ramp was. There was no barrier to stop the car. If we ignored proper braking procedures, the car would roll off the tracks. It would not run off the end of the dock, but would appear so.

We were beginning a run and had added a little extra power between the house and the warehouse, to accelerate our descent on the incline and give us a faster roll down the dock. We were breezing along, laughing and yelling, consumed with delight. When I began to apply the brake, the two-by-four broke in two! All the glee abruptly turned to silence, but only for a split second, because at this juncture it appeared as if we were going to roll right off the end of the dock. The screaming then became deafening. I quickly sat down and put my foot against the stub of the two-by-four, applying pressure with all my might. The car began to slow down. As it slowed enough for safe departure, all my friends departed, leaping off onto the dock. With the load gone, I managed to stop the car just as the tracks ran out!

Needless to say, we didn't ride the Dummy Line anymore that day, but I'll always remember how my pals deserted that sinking ship. I can see them now, in my mind's eye, squalling, tumbling, rolling, and sliding all over that dock after jumping off the moving car.

View of the house from the Dummy Line. Photo courtesy of U.S. National Park Service.

During the Civil War, the fort was used to house prisoners of war, members of the New York 64th and 79th Regiments captured at the first Battle of Manassas (Bull Run). Confederate soldiers pose on the ramparts while the prisoners stand below.

He said, "What did you do that for?" I said, "I gigged a shark!" He yelled, "A shark!" I don't know how he did it, but he got back in that bateau so fast it seemed as though some supernatural power had just lifted him up.

SHARK IN THE SLOUGH

Early one summer morning, a very close friend and I decided to go crabbing in the slough on the east end of Castle Pinckney. The slough was a tidal basin that retained considerable water at low tide and was an ideal haven for crustaceans.

We loaded our gear in the bateau. It consisted of a dip net and my father's gig. We paddled from the dock up the southern side of Castle Pinckney.

The tide was coming in and the sun had begun to peep over the horizon – just the right kind of day for two good pals to be out in a boat. The water had risen just enough to provide ingress to the slough.

I was standing in the bow of the bateau and my friend was standing in the stern. I had the gig and he had the dip net. We eased along the seaward side, dipping and gigging crabs as we went.

We crossed the end of the slough and began moving along the sand and marsh side, continuing to dip and gig crabs. By this time, we had caught quite a few. The tide had risen and we decided to head back to the dock.

Just then, I noticed a shark about five feet long swimming toward the boat where I was standing. Since I had the gig in my hand, the natural thing to do was ram it into the shark, which I hastily did!

There was a thud! The bateau stopped abruptly and my friend fell overboard. I lost my balance, let go of the gig, and fell down in the boat. I got up as quickly as I could. My friend had surfaced and was hanging on the side of the boat. He said, "What did you do that for?" I said, "I gigged a shark!" He yelled, "A shark!" I don't know how he did it, but he got back in that bateau so fast it seemed as though some supernatural power had just lifted him up.

We never saw the shark or the gig again, nor did we tarry long worrying about it. We grabbed the oars and headed for the dock.

All the way back, I wondered what my father was going to say about my losing his gig.

1930s view of Castle Pinckney at low tide.

1930s view of Castle Pinckney at mid tide.

As I stepped into the water, I glanced down and saw what I thought to be a baby flounder by my foot. I spontaneously rammed the gig home. "Ouch! Owwee, owwee!" Pain, pain, pain! I had gigged myself in the foot!

A "GIGGED" FOOT

At Castle Pinckney, the scene was always changing. This, of course, is true of any island or shoreline area. The changes occur with the movement of the tide.

Each time the water receded, it exposed things visible only during the ebb. Each time the tide flowed, it concealed things until the next ebb. At times, the water was calm, serene and tranquil. But, it was subject to elemental influences. A slight breeze would cause a ripple effect. Soft winds would cause a wavy effect. Stronger winds would cause white caps and create a bi-colored image. Very strong winds would cause turmoil and make the harbor seem to boil. When it rained lightly, it looked like millions of minnows jumping up and down. When it rained heavily, it looked like a million little simultaneous explosions taking place. Of all the things at Castle Pinckney to arouse interest, desire, or curiosity, the tide was by far the most intriguing.

The tide and I became fast friends. It ebbed and flowed twice every twenty- four hours. It had its own timetable, never repeating its degree of elevation or recession at the same time on consecutive days. It always brought presents when it came in, such as crabs, fish, and other forms of sea life. Those were standard, daily tidal gifts. The surprise presents were to be found in the marsh and along the beaches. Each time I went exploring, I knew there would be rewards – caps, towels, dungarees, shirts, shoes, boxes, fishing gear, and on and on. You can't imagine the loot I'd bring home!

Each time I'd see the big white banana boats come into the harbor, I knew I'd struck pay dirt. I'd watch them as they came around Fort Ripley Shoal and through the channel paralleling East Battery on their way to the docking slips.

During the unloading process, clumps of green bananas would fall overboard. The tide would deliver them to Castle Pinckney. I would retrieve them in my explorations, take them home, rinse them off, dry them, and put them on a darkened shelf in the pantry where they would ripen. No shortage of potassium at our house!

Once, "friend tide" brought a whole stalk of bananas. It was all I could do to get it to the house, but I managed. It was really fun washing it off and getting it ready for the pantry. In a few days, the bananas were ripe. That time, we nearly "went bananas" trying to eat all of them before they turned black!

In those days, some folks believed the moon influenced the tide. I didn't know about that, but I could look at the moon and pretty well tell the stage of the tide. I knew that when the moon was on the horizon, the tide was high, and when the moon was overhead, the tide was low. The position of the moon gave an instant indication of the tide.

At "dead low" water, a large flat sandy beach graced the front and rear areas of Castle Pinckney. As the tide took its trip to sea, it would leave a variety of depressions, like large basins, filled with sea water. Often, the basins would have a crab or two, or a shrimp or two, or sometimes a small fish trapped until the next tidal cycle.

Also at this time, thousands of "China Back" fiddlers would depart the marsh, join the army and march in procession toward the water's edge. These were the jewels the sheepshead considered a delicacy. I'd take my bucket and fill it up with bait. They were easy to catch. I'd run around and around a regiment several times and they would become confused, start to mill, and dig in. Then I would cup my hands and scoop them together. The usual result -- a double handful of fiddlers. I don't recall ever getting pinched using that procedure.

Each time I would explore the beaches at low tide, I'd take a dip net or a gig or a bucket or some combination. Most frequently, I took my little four-pronged frog gig. As I was walking along the sands, I'd wade through each basin as I came to it. I'd look very carefully for any form of sea life.

One day, as I approached one rather large, interesting basin, I thought, "Man, I'll bet there's something in there." As I stepped into the water, I glanced down and saw what I thought to be a baby flounder by my foot. I spontaneously rammed the gig home. "Ouch! Owwee, owwee!" Pain, pain, pain! I had gigged myself in the foot! One prong had penetrated the fleshy top side of my foot and was sticking out beyond the barb on the bottom of my foot. "Owwee, owwee!" I "owweed" all the way to the house, raising and lowering the gig in time with my stride. It was comical to be walking along with the gig handle going up and down every time I took a step, but I didn't think it was very funny. I was "owweeing"

too much to laugh.

Upon arriving at the house, I distressed my mother with my predicament. She said, "I'll have to pull it out." I cringed, "Owwee, owwee." I said, "You can't, because of the barb. Owwee, owwee!"

I had previously seen my father remove a fish hook from his finger by taking a pair of pliers and cutting the shank in two. Then he pulled the hook out by the point with the nose of the pliers. It was as easy as pie!

I told my mother, "Get Daddy's pliers." She did and I tried Daddy's method. As I carefully placed the cutting edge of the pliers across the tine of the gig, I began to clamp down on the handles to cut it in two. "Owwee, owwee!" I was not strong enough to apply the necessary pressure to cut the tine. My mother tried and she could not cut it. We had made a pretty good indentation in the tine, however, and decided that if we could bend it back and forth, it might snap.

With the pliers, I grasped the tine right at the indentation while my mother moved the gig handle to the right and back to the left. "Owwee, owwee, owwee!" Each time there was motion, there was pain. Suddenly, the tine snapped and all I had now was a gig prong through my foot. "Owwee, owwee!"

I handed my mother the pliers, stuck my foot up in the air and said, "Pull it out." She clamped the pliers on the tine, gave it a yank, and it slid right out. There hadn't been much bleeding up to this point, but when she yanked out that tine, the red began to pour. "Owwee, owwee, owwee!" all over again.

The Ghosts of Castle Pinckney

My mother then went and got the iodine bottle and poured some iodine into the wound. Ouch, burn, fire! "Owwee, owwee, owwee!" She bandaged my foot and in a day or two I was operating as if nothing had happened.

Thinking back, it probably was very amusing to see me walking along raising and lowering that gig between the "Owwees!"

The island during high tide, viewed from the Dummy Line.

Overhead view of structures on Castle Pinckney as it appeared during author's childhood days on the island. (Drawing by author is not to scale.)

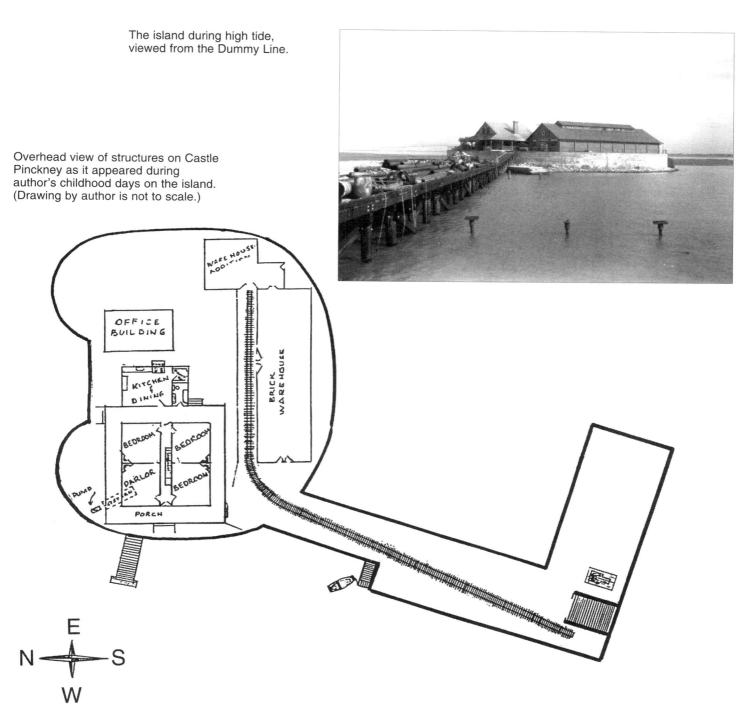

Just then, an idea zipped through my brain: "Get something heavy and drop it on the marsh hen." I ran into the yard and the first thing I saw that would do the trick was a brick.... I took a prone position across the wall, took careful aim and let go of the brick. Bull's eye!

24

A "BRICKEN" NECK

Early one spring morning, we had an unusually high tide. The water, which did not normally rise into the lower yard, had come within a foot of the base of the old fortress wall. The wall was twelve feet high and the top was a concrete walkway like a sidewalk. It had an iron rail around it for safety purposes.

I was up and ready for school, leaning on the rail, waiting for the boat to come. As I pondered the high tide, I wondered how much higher it would rise. All the while, I was peering out across the harbor to see if I could see the boat coming. I could usually see it when it left the Engineer dock. It took about ten minutes to get to Castle Pinckney.

When I saw the boat leave the dock, I began ambling along the walkway toward the end of our dock where we boarded the boat for school. I glanced down and noticed a marsh hen walking along the narrow strip of dry land at the base of the wall. My instant impulse related the marsh hen to the frying pan, so I hurried into the house to get my "410" shot gun. As often happens when the boat is coming and time is of the essence, things don't occur in normal fashion. I could not find any shot gun shells!

Something had to be done in a hurry! The marsh hen might already have disappeared, the boat was getting nearer, and I was in a dither.

Just then, an idea zipped through my brain: "Get something heavy and drop it on the marsh hen." I ran into the yard and the first thing I saw that would do the trick was a brick.

I grabbed it up and sped back to the spot where I had sighted the marsh hen. It was gone! I glanced up and the boat was over halfway from Charleston. Not much time! I began walking around the top of the wall to see if I could see the marsh hen again. Suddenly, I spied it huddled up against the base of the wall with water lapping at its feet.

I eased along the top of the wall until I was directly over the spot where the marsh hen stood. I took a prone position across the wall, took careful aim and let go of the brick. Bull's eye!

I ran down the stairs into the lower yard, sloshing through the water to where the marsh hen lay. I grabbed it up and raced back upstairs and into the kitchen to show my mother what I had bagged. I was about as excited as I could be!

My mother disdainfully exclaimed, "Don't you know, the boat is at the end of the dock waiting on you, and your feet and shoes are soaking wet?"

I dropped the marsh hen in the sink, charged out of the house and went tearing down the wharf to board the boat. The skipper, provoked at me for causing a delay, laughed when I told him I had dropped a brick on a marsh hen.

That afternoon when I came home from school, guess what! My mother had prepared a pan of marsh hen, smothered in gravy. She asked, "How did you kill that marsh hen?" I said, "I guess I 'bricked' its neck!"

Presently, a little dark brown object almost the size of a mouse appeared.... The same little brown furry thing surfaced again. This time, I decided to sit still and observe. The little animal ran about the area of the hole jumping and turning, but not getting very far away.

NINE LITTLE RATS

The yard inside the fortress wall, where our house was located, was rather small. On the right side, from the back porch steps, it was restricted by a concrete wall about fourteen inches high. The wall was actually an extension of the foundation of the warehouse and formed the base for the tracks of the Dummy Line.

One morning, I was sitting on the steps pondering my plan for the day. From the corner of my eye, I thought I detected some kind of motion near the wall. I moved my head to look more directly at the area, but I saw nothing. I thought to myself, "I know I saw something move, so I'll just sit here and watch."

Presently, a little dark brown object almost the size of a mouse appeared. I jumped up and ran over to the wall, but it disappeared in a hole at the base of the wall. I looked at the hole, which did not demonstrate anything spectacular or reveal the presence of life, so I went back to the steps to sit and watch some more.

Not long after that, the same little brown furry thing surfaced again. This time, I decided to sit still and observe. The little animal ran about the area of the hole jumping and turning, but not getting very far away.

My curiosity was beginning to put my brain in the "capture mode." I began to contrive a means to apprehend the little culprit when another one stuck his head from the hole, looked about, and joined his friend.

I thought the old box-stick-and-string snare should do the job, so I began to round up the necessary paraphernalia.

As I did, the two little furry things quickly disappeared into the security of the hole.

I found a small cardboard box, got a little stick about three or four inches long, tied a long piece of fishing line to it and set the trap. It wasn't hard to do. I just placed the box, open-side down, at the wall near the hole. Tilting the box, I propped it up with the little stick. Trailing the fishing line back to the steps, I sat down to see what would happen. In just a little while, the action began. A little brown creature stuck its head from the hole, looked around and bounced out. When it went under the box, I gave the string a yank. Pay dirt! I now had, under the box, whatever it was I was after.

The next thing to do was turn the box up without permitting an escape. How was I going to do that? I thought, perhaps if I could slide a flat piece of cardboard under the box, it would do the job. Off I went in search of a piece of cardboard. I finally found a section large enough and returned to the box fully expecting the prey to be gone.

Carefully, I slid the cardboard under the box, then turned the box over. I eased the cardboard over enough to peep in to see what I had. Imagine my surprise when I beheld a baby wharf rat running around in the box! I put the cardboard back in place and ran to get a bucket to put my "big game" in. I picked up a twelve-quart water pail and returned to the box. Then I thought, "If I put the rat in the pail without a cover, it might jump out."

Off I went again for more equipment. This time, I found a piece of wire mesh with half-inch squares in it. Boy, that was

27

ideal! Now I could get a real good look at the rat and it couldn't get away.

I picked up the box, tilted it so the rat would slide into the pail, and quickly put the wire mesh over the bucket.

At this point, I knew there was at least one more little rat in the hole, so I set up for a repeat performance. What a rewarding venture. Before it was over, I had captured nine little wharf rats. Man, I had really done something!

While I was busy on my trapping expedition, my sisters were in the house. Going up on the porch, I called them to "Come see what I have!"

Like all females, they didn't cotton to rats and ran off to "tell Mama" on me. My mother came out, took a peek, grimaced and said, "Get rid of those nasty things, but don't turn them loose." Get rid of them, but don't turn them loose! That seemed like some kind of double talk.

Besides, I wanted to keep them for "pets."

I took the bucket full of rats around to the porch on the wharf side of the house. I got some bread and stuck it through the wire mesh and they began to nibble away. It was fun watching them eat.

By this time, it was noon and mother called us to come to the kitchen for lunch. As we sat at the table, all I wanted to talk about were my rats. I soon found out in a most forceful way that rats aren't a very suitable subject for dining conversation.

After eating, I went back to see how my rats were. Well, I got the surprise of my life! The bucket was turned over, the wire mesh was off, and the rats were gone.

Remember the earlier story about cats? I think that while I was having lunch, so were the cats!

Prisoners' quarters No.1, dubbed "Hotel Zouave" for the 69th New York Fire Zouaves imprisoned there.

The Ghosts of Castle Pinckney

Confederate officers and enlisted men posed together for this group portrait. Photo courtesy of U.S. National Park Service.

Charleston Zouave cadets, lead by Lt. R. C. Gilchrist, pose before the walls of Castle Pinckney. Photo courtesy of U.S. National Park Service.

It was a monster, the kind people tell stories about the rest of their days, and little boys dream about every time they see a China Back fiddler. My father took the fish to Charleston. It was frozen in a block of ice, and placed on display in the window of a King Street restaurant for all to see.

A BIG SHEEPSHEAD

We moved to Castle Pinckney during the Great Depression. Not long afterward, an adult family friend came to live with us for a while. He was out of a job, had no family that we knew of, and was all but destitute.

A very fine man with polished manners, he was a gentleman in every sense of the word. His influence on us children was wholesome. He spoke excellent English and his diction was clear and distinct. He shared with us the importance of good speech habits.

One of the most memorable things about him was his musical ability. He was an accomplished violinist and frequently played his fiddle for us. I recall fondly the entertainment he provided with his recurring concerts.

At Castle Pinckney, he became a skilled and ardent fisherman and spent much time practicing the art. His specialty was catching sheepshead.

This particular species of fish was rather abundant and thrived around the pilings, rocks, oyster banks or anywhere there were oysters, barnacles or other crustaceans. The Charleston jetties have always been a haven for them and are visited frequently by fishermen adroit enough to bring them in.

Sheepshead are particularly fond of China Back fiddlers, the little crabs having one large claw and one small claw and a back decorated as if hand-painted in some oriental studio by a master of the art. Close inspection reveals almost unbelievable color patterns.

We always used fiddlers for bait. They were plentiful and not difficult to catch, but, if one were not careful, the big claw would make him regret it. They pack a powerful pinch!

Catching the bait is easy. Catching the sheepshead is not. They are masters of deception and will consume a fiddler from a hook before you can bat an eye. You can always tell when Mr. Sheepshead has taken your bait because he leaves a calling card – the empty "painted" shell that was once the back of a fiddler.

Sheepshead have a very unusual dental pattern. Looking at the fish head-on, the teeth resemble those of humans. Behind the first row of teeth, the roof and floor of the fish's mouth contain nubby, rounded teeth. These are for crushing oysters, barnacles, or other things the fish may want to feed upon.

Their normal dining procedure is to crush the shell and suck out the edible parts. With the fiddler crab, this is very evident. When baiting the hook, you run the hook from side to side through the shell of the fiddler. When Mr. Sheepshead comes along, he crushes the fiddler with his designer teeth, sucks out all the goodies and goes on his merry way. You are left with the fiddler back intact to let you know he paid a visit.

We learned from experience that there was a secret to catching sheepshead. A long substantial cane pole, a strong line, and proper-sized hook baited with a big China Back fiddler wasn't all it really took, unless you wanted to harvest empty backs all day.

The solution to the mystery of backs on the hook instead of Sheepshead was in the maneuvering of the line. There are two techniques that really get results. One is slowly raising and lowering the pole up and down so the line will move through a vertical distance of six to eight inches. As the fish is biting, you can feel the weight and set the hook. The other technique requires the cooperation of the elements. If water conditions permit, you can watch your line closely at the point where it is in the water. When the fish takes the bait, there is a slight movement of the line. When the line moves, you set the hook. We used both techniques and found the results rewarding. Seldom did we ever come up empty-handed when we went sheepshead fishing.

One afternoon, upon arriving home from school, our fiddling friend (music and bait) met me as I disembarked. He was all agog and said, "Boy, have I got something to show you!" I said, "What is it?" He said, "Wait and see!"

We walked gingerly up the wharf toward the house. He stopped at the point where there were steps extending to the water's edge, which we used to get in and out of the bateau. We also had a large wire-box basket tied there for keeping fish alive. The basket was about three feet long, two feet wide, and eighteen or twenty inches deep.

We proceeded down the steps to where the basket was. By this time, even a fourth grader, like I was, could suspect what he was going to show me. All that excitement and rapid walking just to see a fish! I'd seen plenty of fish!

My anticipation was beginning to wane as he pulled the basket from the water. As the basket began to clear the water, I could readily see the cause for all the excitement.

He hauled it up on the steps and my eyes bulged in disbelief. I gasped! In the basket was the biggest sheepshead I had ever seen. Its broad, prominent black-and-white stripes made it look like a convict in jail. The fish was enormous. My friend said, "How many fiddlers do you suppose he has eaten?" I said, "I don't know, except the last one!"

The big fish weighed thirteen pounds and five ounces. It was a monster, the kind people tell stories about the rest of their days, and little boys dream about every time they see a China Back fiddler.

My father took the fish to Charleston. It was frozen in a large block of ice and placed on display in the window of a King Street restaurant for all to see.

The Ghosts of Castle Pinckney

Another view of the barracks, upper and lower floors. Also notice the hot shot furnace in the lower left hand quarter of the picture.

Post Civil War photo showing stacks of cannon balls. Note the 10" Columbiad cannon on the carriage in the background.

I dropped my line in the water.... Presently, Mr. Sheepshead came slowly around the piling. When he saw that fiddler, he nosed into it, opened his mouth and pulled it ever so gently away from the piling. At that moment, I set the hook.

A FISH FOR SUNDAY DINNER

Though Castle Pinckney was a kind of paradise, it was not without some drawbacks. We had no electricity. We cooked on a wood stove, and studied by the light from kerosene lamps. Our only modern convenience at the time was a telephone in the office maintained by the Corps of Engineers. We had an access key to the office if ever the need arose to make a call. Incoming calls were almost non-existent.

Not only were we isolated in the middle of the harbor, but our nation was engulfed in the Great Depression. It was tough going, very tough, all over the country. Money was scarce and many families barely eked out a survival. Even bare necessities such as groceries were hard to come by.

My mother usually went grocery shopping biweekly, depending on how much money we had. She would stock up on staples and canned goods. She could not stock up on perishables as we had no means of preservation. We had an ice box, but it was a joke. It was designed to hold a fifty-pound block of ice in the top compartment. The bottom compartment, where food was stored, was only about twice the size of the ice compartment. You really couldn't keep much meat, butter, milk or the like very long. Besides, the horse-drawn ice wagons that roamed the streets of Charleston never came by our door. It was a rare thing to have ice. When we did, even a glass of ice water was a treat.

We frequently found our pantry in a state of diminished supply. My mother reminded me of "the old woman who lived in a shoe" – often when she went to the pantry, the pantry was bare.

One Sunday morning at breakfast, she said, "You children eat heartily this morning because I don't know what we're going to have for dinner."

My wheels began to turn. I contemplated the situation and wondered what I could do to help. Thinking, "Maybe I can catch a fish big enough for dinner," I went and got my pole and some China Back fiddlers and ambled down the dock.

The tide was high, a position we called "top of the flood." This was the period when the flow had ceased and the ebb was about to begin. The water looked like an enormous sheet of glass covering the entire harbor. Not normally the best time for fishing, but I knew that sheepshead were prone to feed at high tide. They feasted on the succulent barnacles attached to the pilings but not submerged except at high tide.

I edged along the side of the dock and peered down at the pilings to see if I could spot a big one. You could always see them in their black-and-white-striped outfits, glimmering in the clear water as they swam around the pilings, crushing and eating barnacles.

My intention was to go down one side of the wharf, cross the end and come back up the other side. At the end of the wharf, there was a loading ramp built on about a thirty-degree incline. As I eased down the ramp, I reaped my reward. There, feeding around an adjacent piling, was a big one. I almost lost my breath, gulped a few times and thought, "Gollee!"

I put a fiddler on my hook and eased

my pole under the top of the wharf. Then, timing it when the fish was on the opposite side of the piling, I dropped my line in the water. I guided it carefully so that it would drift up against the barnacles on the piling and place the fiddler in the "table is set" mode.

Presently, Mr. Sheepshead came slowly around the piling. When he saw that fiddler, he nosed into it, opened his mouth and pulled it ever so gently away from the piling.

At that moment, I set the hook. My pole banged against the top of the dock and I stumbled backwards, holding on with all my might. It's hard to imagine the scene. There I was, stumbling off balance, on a thirty-degree declining ramp, a cracked pole in my hand, a big sheepshead on the line, wondering whether I was going to go swimming or catch a fish.

I recovered instantly and began a hand-over-hand recovery of the pole and line. The sheepshead was staging a gallant fight. When I got to the point where I ran out of pole and could catch the line, I grabbed it. It was all I could do to pull it in. Just as I landed the sheepshead on the ramp, the hook came out of his mouth! He fluttered all over the ramp. I thought for sure he was a goner.

I pounced on him with all fours. The big dorsal fin penetrated deep into the inside of my thigh. Ouch! It really began to sting! Ignoring the pain, I got my fingers in his gills and held on. It was a struggle to keep from sliding down the ramp into the water, but I had caught the fish!

With hand in gill, I abandoned the pole and line and, with *summa-cum-laude* glee, trotted up the wharf to show Mama what we would have for dinner. She was as thrilled as I was.

Aerial view of Castle Pinckney, much as it looked during the time the author's family lived on the island. Photo courtesy of U.S. National Park Service.

The Ghosts of Castle Pinckney

Engraving of Castle Pinckney, circa 1800s.

Photo of Castle Pinckney taken in 1993.

I landed in a heap, striking my chin on the sharp edge of one of the barnacles. The blow dazed me and put a large ugly gash on my chin. When I lost my balance and began to fall, I yelled, attracting the attention of the others.

A FALL FROM THE DOCK

Summertime was always the greatest season at Castle Pinckney. We had a house full of relatives and friends most of the time and every day was a party.

Crabbing was a favorite thing to do, so we children usually kept up with the tidal movement. We learned that sea life flowed and ebbed with the tide. We didn't have, nor did we need, tide tables. We were situated in the center of the seafood "land of milk and honey." We could tell at a glance when the tide was right. This applied to crabbing, oystering, fishing, gigging, catching fiddlers, and to any of the other phenomena related to tidal flow.

One thing that made Castle Pinckney such a Utopia was that most of the activity involved the pursuit and harvest of seafood. The delight always peaked at meal time. Each time we would sit down to feast upon the spoils of our effort, there were always related tales to share, like "the one that got away," or "if you knew how to use a dip net, we'd have caught more crabs."

One summer, as Old Sol was beaming over the jetties and down on the still harbor waters, a group of us children was getting our crabbing lines ready for an assault on the crustacea. The tide had ebbed at about 8:30 a.m., which meant that, between nine and eleven, the clear harbor waters would be "crawling" with the prey we sought.

On this particular occasion, several of our cousins were in the group. One was sixteen and had Red Cross Lifesaver certification. We thought that placed her in a "protection" category, so we decided to explore a new crabbing territory.

The men from the Corps of Engineers had tied up an old lighter on the Charleston side of the Castle Pinckney wharf. We thought it would be ideal for crabbing. The barge was flat on top and provided four-sided access to the water. It sat low in the water, which facilitated dipping up the crabs as we pulled in our lines. Besides, if anyone fell overboard, our older cousin could do the lifesaving.

We assembled our crab lines, dip nets, a bushel basket and extra bait, then took off for the lighter. We were charged with exuberance as we hurried down the wharf. We engineered the transfer from the wharf to the lighter without mishap and hastened to get our lines in the water.

The crabs were very active and in just a little time we had the bushel basket nearly full. They were beginning to crawl out, so I climbed back up on the wharf to go to the house and find a basket lid.

On the way back to the lighter, I was walking near the edge of the incline of the wharf. The incoming water was just beginning to reach the granite retaining wall that formed a jetty around the perimeter of the lower-level yard. I was looking to see if I could spot any crabs in the shallow water. I leaned a little too far, lost my balance and fell head first from the wharf to the water's-edge side of the barnacle-laden rocks below, a distance of about ten feet. I landed in a heap, striking my chin on the sharp edge of one of the barnacles. The blow dazed me and put a large ugly gash in my chin.

When I lost my balance and began to fall, I yelled, attracting the attention of the others. My older cousin, the one with the lifesaver training, spontaneously dove into the water and swam as fast as she could to where I was. When she reached me, I was a bloody mess, and just regaining my senses. The blood was oozing down my neck and over my chest. She got me to my feet. By this time, my accident had drawn a crowd. Everyone in the crabbing party deserted the lighter and gathered around me in a state of juvenile curiosity.

My older cousin led me across the rocks into the lower yard and up the stairs to the house-level. When we reached the front porch, my aunt met us and asked, "What on earth has happened?"

A little blood goes a long way and, since I had been bleeding profusely for eight to ten minutes, I presented a rather "sanguine" picture. My aunt became nauseated at all the blood and said, "I think I am going to faint." She realized, however, that this was an emergency and no time to stage a production, but she did gag a few times.

We went back to the kitchen and she placed a clean washcloth over the cut under my chin. Applying pressure with one hand to diminish the blood flow, she began to wash me off with the other. After successfully getting the blood flow reduced and my chin cleaned up, I didn't look too bad. She took me to the bedroom and told me to lie down, which I did. My aunt then proceeded to scorch handkerchiefs with a hot iron to make sterile compresses for the wound.

Conveniences were limited back in those days. We didn't enjoy the luxury of electricity. It was necessary to fire up the old wood stove in the kitchen to heat the flat irons to sterilize the handkerchiefs. Our first aid kit consisted of a bottle of iodine. What a burn! When my aunt located that gem, she thought she had graduated from med school! I thought she was going to kill me!

My mother, taking advantage of my aunt's visit, had gone to Charleston on the morning boat to do some shopping. After some effort, my aunt located her by telephone and related the details of the incident. She told my mother that she was sure the gash required stitches. They decided that I should go to Charleston for medical attention. My aunt got me dressed presentably, and my older cousin and I were soon headed for the city.

My mother was waiting at the dock when we arrived. She took me directly to the emergency room where the doctor examined, stitched, and bandaged the wound. With my new "white beard," we headed back to the Engineer dock in time to catch the last boat back to the Castle.

Everyone seemed glad to see me. They were eager to tell me that all of the crabs that could crawl out of the basket did, but they had boiled and picked the rest of them. For supper, we had grits and crab patties, a gourmet combination.

It wasn't much fun watching them dine so enjoyably when I couldn't even move my jaw! Although they treated me like a hero, I felt more like a "fall guy."

The Ghosts of Castle Pinckney

A group of officers in full-dress uniform lined up for these photos. Evidently, more than one pose was necessary.

View of the warehouse from the Dummy Line. Photo courtesy of U.S. National Park Service.

Soon, we were beginning to feel a little funny, giggling and laughing. My older sister said, "Let's go taste it again." We went back to the pantry and "tasted" the wine a few more times. The more we tasted, the funnier it got. Stumbling was soon added to the giggling and laughter.

A TASTE OF RAISIN WINE

We had a daily run of three boat trips between Castle Pinckney and Charleston. The time schedule for departing the Engineer dock in Charleston was 8:00 a.m., 2:30 p.m., and 4:30 p.m.

The morning run brought the Corps of Engineer workmen to the island and took us to school on the return trip. The 2:30 run brought supplies and equipment and supervisory personnel. It also brought us home from school. The 4:30 run brought my father home and took the workmen back to the city.

Occasionally, my mother would go to the city on the 2:30 boat to shop a while and return on the 4:30 boat. One particular afternoon, her absence became the occasion for disobedience and hilarity.

She had decided to make some homemade raisin wine, something completely foreign to us kids. We watched as she selected the ingredients and went through the preparation. Necessarily, wine has to go through the fermenting process. This was explained to us as she stored the wine in the dark recesses of the pantry, but we didn't understand "ferment."

We didn't know anything about wine. We had never seen it made, had never tasted it, and couldn't imagine anything about the outcome. We did know that our curiosity was increasing day by day during the fermentation.

I don't recall the length of time required for fermentation, but days and days passed. We children, for whatever reason, grew exceedingly impatient with the delay. We wondered what our involvement would be when the wine was ready. Of course, we were not supposed to be involved, but we didn't know that.

My mother was going to Charleston on the 2:30 boat one day, during the fermenting process, to run a few errands and do some shopping. As she was departing, she admonished us, "Be good, and don't bother the wine." Now, she set the stage – she would be in Charleston, we three children would be home alone, instructed to "be good."

I suppose that, in our minds, "being good" and "bothering the wine" were not analogous, so, when the boat cast off, we headed directly for the pantry. From the shelf, we took one of the jars with the wire clip on it. When we released the clip, the top blew open. No way to keep "bothering the wine" a secret now! The pantry smelled like a winery. We grabbed some dish towels and began cleaning up as best we could. Then, we wondered where to hide the dish towels. The odor was very strong, but it sure smelled good!

We decided to take just a taste of what was left in the half-gallon mason jar. My older sister was first. She tried it and said, "It tastes good!" Then, she handed me the jar. I tasted it and agreed with her. I handed the jar to my younger sister. She whimpered and said, "I don't want to get a spanking." I said, "Taste it!" She did.

It was very sweet and, though there was something unusual mixed in with the "sweet," we had quite a few sips. We left the jar in the pantry and went out to play. Soon, we were beginning to feel a little funny, giggling and laughing. My older sister said, "Let's go taste it again."

We went back to the pantry and "tasted" the wine a few more times. The more we tasted, the funnier it got. Stumbling was soon added to the giggling and laughter.

Soon, our mother came home. She found three of the happiest kids she had ever seen. The first thing she said was, "What on earth is the matter with you?" We could not hide the truth. My older sister, with slurred and giggly speech, said, "We tathted the wine."

My mother gasped, "Oh, my Lord, didn't I tell you not to bother the wine?" We all said, "Yeth muwham," and she burst into laughter. Then, she composed herself and said sternly, "Go to the bedroom and stay there 'til I call you."

We went reeling off to the bedroom, where we giggled and laughed some more. By and by, we drifted off to sleep. No supper for disobedient kids!

Troops standing at attention outside the fort.

The Ghosts of Castle Pinckney

Prisoners of war in barracks No. 2, a converted casemate (gun emplacement), appear to be a mixture of nautical personnel and infantry.

View from the front of the fort. Photo courtesy of U. S. National Park Service.

"MY" CREEK

The little creek that curved its way into the depths of the marsh at Castle Pinckney was a favorite haunt of mine. Many times, I'd get in the bateau and paddle up and down the creek just to pass some time away. There was an ever-present intrigue to that creek. I claimed it for my very own. I can't recall anyone else ever being in that creek unless I was with them. It was, for all intents and purposes, "my" creek.

I once saw a large porpoise in the creek. I guess he thought I was going to try to trap him as I paddled in. It didn't take him long to decide what he was going to do! In a split second, he "poured on the coal" and came sailing by the bateau, ninety miles an hour, so close I could have touched him. He was really moving! He disturbed the water so much it rocked the bateau.

Another time, I found a little wooden jon boat that had run away from home and drifted into the recesses of the marsh up the creek. It was one of those little skiffs, about four feet long and two feet wide at the beam, reminiscent of the ones we boys would put in at Colonial Lake and enjoy paddling around, a type obviously created by some aspiring marine engineer. I tried to resurrect it, but it was too far gone.

At low tide, I used to walk across the beach to the creek and fish for minnows. There was just a trickle of flow at the last of the ebb. Minnows, by the hundreds, congregated in the little basin area at the mouth of the creek.

I used a real fancy rig to catch minnows. It consisted of a straight pin, about six feet of #50 sewing thread and a branch from an oleander bush. A pair of pliers would curl the point of a pin into the neatest minnow hook you ever saw. Mother did a great deal of sewing, so there was plenty of line available. Lining the front of the house were large, colorful oleander bushes, so poles were no problem to obtain.

Minnows will try to eat anything small enough to get their mouth on, so bait was abundant. My favorite bait was fatback. I'd cut a small slab of fatback and dice it into little cubes about an eighth of an inch thick. It was white, visible in the water, and the minnows loved it.

Standing on the bank, I would flip my little fatback-baited pin-hook out into the water with my oleander pole. There would be an instant surge of minnows. The pole would bend a little and I'd get a hint of a bite. As this occurred, I'd give the pole a snatch and here would come a big mud.

Catching minnows was so much fun! I'd take a twelve-quart pail with me. By the time the incoming tide began to bring a fresh supply of water into the creek, I'd have a bucket full. I always partially filled the bucket with creek water so the minnows would stay alive. When the incoming tidal current began to accelerate, the fishing would be done, so I'd pour the minnows back in the creek and head for the house.

I often went fishing or crabbing in the creek. I'd use shrimp for bait to catch croakers, whiting, yellow tails, spot-tail bass and other varieties. I hated catching catfish and toadfish. They were difficult to get off the hook. Besides, a catfish would "fin" you and a toadfish would "bite" you. You had to be very careful removing the hook from the mouth.

Crabs were something else. I could almost fill the boat every time I went crabbing. Sometimes, I'd stay in the creek until the tide ebbed all the way. I'd anchor the bateau at the mouth of the creek and walk back to the house for something to eat and drink. When I had my fill, I'd return to the creek and continue whatever activity the stage of the tide permitted.

Catching shrimp was a challenge. I didn't have a cast net. I did have one of those circular drop nets with the conical netting. I'd tie bait in the bottom of the net and lower it into the water. The net would collapse on the bottom as the rim came to rest. Waiting a short spell, I would abruptly raise the net from the water, catching several shrimp. There were always more than that in the net, but they'd back out in a streak as I put the net in motion during the elevation process.

One day, I dreamed up a remedy to prevent shrimp from escaping the net. I took a section of quarter-inch wire cable and fashioned a hoop a little larger than the hoop on the drop net. My hoop would extend beyond the net hoop when lowered into the water.

I took an old burlap bag and cut a twelve-inch strip from it. I got some fishing line and stitched the burlap to the hoop on the drop net. This created a wall section. I stitched the top of the wall section to the hoop I had made. I then tied a drop line to the top hoop. Bravo! Now, I had a drop net with walls to deter escaping shrimp.

I didn't want to wait to try it out, but I had to because the tide was not right. It wasn't temperamental. You just had to be patient and schedule your timing to

For added safety against brick hit by enemy shellfire becoming additional shrapnel, Castle Pinckney was converted into an earthwork by burying its masonry walls. Even today, the fort is still largely filled with sand. Photo courtesy of U. S. National Park Service.

coincide with the tide's timing.

The tide eventually moved into the shrimping mode. Tying bait in my imagination, I set off down the dock to experiment. I was almost dancing with anticipation.

I lowered the new rig into the water at a depth of about three feet. The burlap collapsed around the netting as it settled on the bottom. I waited, patiently, then quickly raised the net. Hallelujah! Hallelujah! It worked! It worked!

Trapped in the net were more shrimp than I had ever caught at one time. Ten or twelve big shrimp were jumping about. I put them in a bucket and lowered the net again. Repeat performance. By the time the tide moved through its course and out of shrimping range, I'd caught an abundance of magnificent shrimp. My day was made! I had a new invention to take with me on my creek.

One day, about midmorning, I was paddling to my creek to catch some crabs. The water was clear and the air was still and refreshing.

At the mouth of the creek, on the left side, was a rather large oyster bed. On the opposite side was a small, sandy beach. When the tide was about halfway into the rise, the oyster bed was submerged in about two feet of water.

As I paddled into the mouth of the creek, a dark object about the size of a saucer caught my eye. It was moving slowly through the water over the oyster bed, about a foot below the surface. On closer inspection, I recognized it as a diamond-back terrapin! In all my days at Castle Pinckney, I had never seen one, although they inhabit Southern marshlands.

I dove over the side of the bateau and began swimming like crazy in chase of the terrapin. To my utter delight, I caught it! It was beautiful! Shades of dark and light green with diamond-shaped decoration. I spun around in the water, with terrapin in hand, to swim back to the bateau. To my amazement, the bateau was gone.

When I excitedly dove over the side, I must have given it a shove with my foot, propelling it into the current, as it had drifted upstream. I spied it at the first bend of the creek, about sixty feet away.

Here I am trying to hold on to a gleaming trophy turtle which is scratching and wriggling to get away. I'm struggling to stay afloat and now I've got to swim after an elusive bateau! Well, I made it and also managed to hang on to the terrapin! I put it in the bottom of the bateau, climbed over the side, and beamed with delight as I watched it crawl about while I paddled back to the wharf.

When I got to the house, I was anxious to show off my catch to my mother and sisters. The spectacular natural design and the distinctive markings on its shell were intriguing.

I put it in a large galvanized tub half-filled with seawater. Now, I would have a beautiful little pet to feed and play with.

However, my pleasure was short-lived. When my father came home, he was pleased and amused at my catch. He then proceeded to burst my balloon! He said, "Son, diamond-back terrapins are protected by law. You'll have to turn it loose." He "cudda" lived a long time without saying that!

Suddenly, I came upon a baby diamondback terrapin crawling in the marsh mud. I reached down quickly and picked it up…. The little turtle was a tad smaller than the painted variety you could purchase at Schaidereses on Meeting and Wentworth Streets.

A BABY DIAMONDBACK TERRAPIN

My playground at Castle Pinckney included the backyard around the perimeter of the old fortress wall, the wide beaches at low tide behind and in front of the "Castle," the slough on the back side toward Mt. Pleasant, and the thirteen acres of marsh area. The old wharf was also a prime attraction.

On any given day, especially in warm weather, one might find me in any of these areas. There were always crawling things to see, swimming things to look for, flying things to observe, ships to watch entering and leaving the harbor, and a host of small boats always in motion by sail, motor, or oar, traversing the broad expanse of beautiful water.

Bogging out through the marshy area near the slough one morning, I was all alone having a big time entertaining myself. Suddenly, I came upon a baby diamondback terrapin crawling in the marsh mud. I reached down quickly and picked it up. The find was exhilarating, reminiscent of another episode with a diamond-back!

It didn't take me long to conclude my exploration for the day. I hurried back to the house, on "cloud nine" the whole way. The little turtle was a tad smaller than the painted variety you could purchase at Schaidereses on Meeting and Wentworth Streets.

I couldn't get to the house quickly enough. I was anxious to get my baby diamond-back in a safe place as well as show it off.

I put him in an empty goldfish bowl, dipped up some sea-water and filled the bowl about one-third full. I then placed a small piece of weathered wood in the aquarium so the little turtle could crawl out of the water and sun himself.

I fed him little bits of cooked fish. It was fun watching him eat. As the bit of fish would submerge, the little "terp" would swim over and bite it. He would then take his front leg, extend the claws and scratch away the excess, leaving a tasty morsel in his mouth to munch on.

I was so happy about that little gem! I took it to school to show all the third-graders in my class what a diamond-back terrapin looked like. It surely did go over big with all the children; however, I think the teacher was the most impressed.

She told me to place the bowl on the window ledge where everyone could see it. Presently, she went over to where the bowl was, turned to the class and directed the students to come in groups of four from each row to see the little diamond-back terrapin Eddie brought in.

She carefully reached in and picked up the little turtle, then proceeded to explain and describe his features, markings, and characteristics in detail to each group. Amazingly, she seemed to know everything about diamond-back terrapins. Also, I was busting at the seams. It was such a wonderful "show and tell" experience and I had brought the whole "show!"

Not long afterward, I returned the little turtle to the marsh. It, too, was protected by the law.

I knew that time was critical
if I was going to get it into the water
and around to the wharf. The boat was full
of water. I tried hard to tilt it enough to spill
the water, but I just wasn't strong enough.
Neither could I drag it into the slough. I
needed help! Lickety-split, I set out
for the house.

THE DAY I FOUND THE "IF"

Explorations at Castle Pinckney were never as exciting as after a storm. Strong winds would usually blow all kinds of interesting things up in the marsh and on the beaches.

One morning, after the departure of a series of raging nocturnal boomers, I was out on the porch looking around, trying to decide which way I would go first. Going exploring was a foregone conclusion. Where to begin was up for grabs. Anticipation was peaking! As I glanced about, I noticed on the back of the island what appeared to be the mast of a boat on the bank of the slough.

When I spied that object, I immediately decided to head out to determine just what it was. I waded along the beach, at the edge of the marsh, toward the slough.

The closer I came to the object, the more detail I could envision. As I rounded the point where the marsh ended and the slough began, looming before me, several hundred feet away, was a one-masted sailboat. It was high and dry on the shell bank.

Responding to an invisible spurt of acceleration, I put everything into high gear. With tension mounting and eyes aglow, I darted toward the boat.

It surely was a sail boat, approximately eight feet long, four feet wide, with one mast, and the sail neatly furled and secured. It even had a centerboard. I beamed as I looked it over. On the transom, there were two big red letters, "IF." As with everything else I ever found, my first reaction was to take it to the house.

The tide was well into the ebb, having receded a little beyond the halfway mark. I knew that time was critical if I was going to get it in the water and around to the wharf. The boat was full of water. I tried hard to tilt it enough to spill the water, but I just wasn't strong enough. Neither could I drag it into the slough. I needed help!

Lickety-split, I set out for the house. My older sister had a friend visiting her and I began calling them as soon as I was near enough for them to hear me. They soon came around the rear of the warehouse and into view. "What's the matter?" my sister yelled. I pointed in the direction of the sailboat and yelled back, "Y'all come and help me get it in the water and we'll bring it to the dock. Hurry up, too. The tide's going out!"

They came hastily and we were soon at the boat side, straining to tilt it up so the water would run out. Our efforts paid off and enabled us to get most of the water out. Then came the task of dragging it about thirty feet to the water.

We pushed and tugged and pulled and twisted and performed just about every contortion imaginable, finally managing to get the "IF" afloat. Whew! What a relief! All three of us felt like collapsing.

Water in the slough at this time was about three feet deep in the middle. The little boat didn't draw much water and we waded along pulling and pushing the new prize.

Rounding the point of the marsh, we headed toward the wharf. We were navigating very well until we neared the wharf. We had no paddles. Our only means of propulsion was by hand and foot. We needed to circumnavigate the wharf because the fixed mast was too tall to allow passage underneath. The water was becoming too deep to wade, so the three of us climbed aboard. I sat on the stern with my feet dangling in the water, kicking for all I was worth. My sister and her friend sat side-by-side amidships and paddled with their hands. After much exertion, we succeeded in getting to the end of the wharf. Little did we imagine the impending disaster.

As we rounded the end of the wharf and came into the open water, we realized that our means of propulsion was ineffective against the ebbing currents. At this point, panic prevailed and we began yelling and screaming for Mama.

Fortunately, she heard us and came running out onto the dock to see what was going on. What she saw had a built-in heart attack potential for her. She yelled excitedly, "I'll call the Coast Guard!" and raced out of sight.

There we were, three kids on a prize yacht, adrift in Charleston harbor, on the strong, outgoing tide, heading for the Atlantic Ocean! It really doesn't get much better than that! Or worse, depending on your perspective.

We resigned ourselves to the predicament, comfortable in the knowledge that the Coast Guard would soon be coming to pick us up. My sister then began this tirade that it was all my fault, that I had no business bothering the boat in the first place, and she'd never help me again! Her friend chimed in with, "My mother would die if she knew where I was!"

My mother now had come down to the end of the dock. She stood there nervously as two of her children and one of someone else's sat helpless, ocean-bound, on an unknown vessel. By this time, we had drifted beyond earshot, so there was no communication.

When we tilted the boat earlier, you recall, we were unable to get all the water out. It suddenly dawned on us that the water in the boat was deepening and there was a good possibility that it might sink. That realization reactivated the panic button. We contemplated jumping overboard and swimming to safety. The shore by this time, at the nearest point, was about a quarter of a mile away. My sister and her friend had about decided to do just that when we saw, in the distance, a boat coming from the city.

It seemed like an eternity was passing. Finally, the boat came near enough for us to determine it was not the Coast Guard. Talk about frantic! We began waving and yelling and screaming to attract attention!

The boat maneuvered up to where we were. There were two men on board. One of them asked, "Do you kids need some help?" "Humph!" I felt like saying, "No, we're out here for lunch," but my sister spoke up spontaneously and said, "We sure do! We were waiting for the Coast Guard."

The man looked at the boat, now almost full of water and looked at the furled sail. With puzzled consternation, he asked, "Is something wrong with your sail?" I spoke up and said, "No, sir, none of us knows how to sail. We just found this boat!" He asked, "Where do you live?" I said, "Castle Pinckney," and pointed toward home. He said, "Throw me a rope and we'll tow you in." I said, "We don't have a rope." He mumbled under his breath, probably something like, "You don't have a lick of sense, either!"

Going into the cabin, he came back with a section of rope. He asked, disdainfully, "Can you tie a knot?" I said, boastfully, "Yes, sir, I can tie a bowline!" He wasn't impressed. He said, "Tie up and we'll tow you in."

They were laughing and seemed amused at our predicament as they towed us to the wharf. Once safe, we expressed our gratitude for the rescue. My mother, in tears, said to the men, "I can't thank you enough! The phone was dead and I couldn't reach the Coast Guard." It's a good thing we kids didn't know that. We'd have "died" for sure.

Several days after this exciting episode, we learned that the boat belonged to a Mount Pleasant resident whose initials were "IF." Contact was made and the little boat was returned intact to its rightful owner, leaving me with another memorable drama of everyday life at Castle Pinckney.

View of the house and warehouse from the Dummy Line, showing remnants of an earlier dock. Photo courtesy of U.S. National Park Service.

We decided, since we were where we could not see the boat coming, it would be a justifiable reason his for not catching the boat back to the city. He picked up a stone and threw it out into space and gleefully said, "I missed the boat." The boat came and went. He and I never saw it, and the rock also had missed it.

TO TELL THE TRUTH

I learned to row a bateau at a tender age. The summer we moved to Castle Pinckney, I was seven years plus two months old.

Simultaneously with the move came the "King of Bateaux," a little skiff destined to play a prominent role in life at the Castle.

By the time I was ten, I could row easily from the island to the docks in Charleston, a distance of about a mile, plus or minus some, depending on the particular dock site. It was not the least unusual for me to row to the city and bring a friend home with me, or take a friend back to the city, as the case may be.

We preferred to use the scheduled launch trips, however, and did, most of the time. One of my closest friends would have lived with us full-time, had parental consent been attainable. Many times, his mother permitted him to come home from school with me on the 2:30 boat, play until the 4:30 boat, and return to the city.

We used to have so much fun together that parting was painful. It wasn't long into our acquaintanceship before we began to resent being separated. We tried to manipulate our parents into letting us spend more time together.

One Friday afternoon when my pal came home from school with me on the 2:30 boat, we played together intensely. When it was about time for the 4:30 boat to arrive, we decided it would be a "jam-up idea" if he could spend the night! Then we could play all day Saturday and row him to Charleston in the bateau! Yeah!

We went down on the lower yard and walked around back to the Fort Sumter side. He did not want to tell his mother a falsehood, so we concocted a magnificent excuse, one that was couched in the truth but not exactly the whole truth.

We decided, since we were where we could not see the boat coming, it would be a justifiable reason for his not catching the boat back to the city. To add further to this transparent juvenile ruse, he picked up a stone and threw it out into space and gleefully said, "I missed the boat!" The boat came and went. He and I never saw it, and the rock also had missed it.

Now, we headed for the telephone to tell his mother what happened. We just knew we were "home free." He called home. "Mother, may I spend the night at Castle Pinckney? Aw, please! I've been invited and we're having a real good time! Please!.... Well, I have to, because I missed the boat." A brief listening moment and he hung up the phone and hung down his head. I asked, "What did she say?" He replied, "For me to come home right now, even if I have to swim!" Busted play! Head for the oars.

I rowed him to the city so he could get back home without having to swim. While we glided slowly across the harbor, we talked about our plan that went awry. We concluded that "devious honesty" was not the best policy.

My friend whispered, "Shoot him!" The rat paused as if he had heard something. I whispered, "I don't want to shoot him!" The rat began to move. My friend elbowed me forcefully and whispered with authority, "Shoot him!" I raised the rifle, took aim, and fired.

RATS!

My friend (from "To Tell the Truth") lived with his parents and two sisters in an upstairs apartment of a boarding house on Wentworth Street. His mother ran the boarding house.

Food was served "Cafeteria Style," primarily for the convenience of boarders. The cafeteria was also open to the public and was a very popular eatery. Going through the serving line and eating in the dining room was a highlight of each visit.

One Friday evening, I was visiting overnight. We had dined and the cafeteria was closed and secured. My friend said to me, "Guess what we're going to do tonight." "What?" I asked. He said, "We're going to shoot rats!" I said, "Where? I don't want to shoot rats!" Grabbing his single-shot 22-caliber rifle, he said, "In the basement of the cafeteria. Come on!"

By now, it had been dark for some time. We slowly and quietly opened the door and entered the basement. Shelves on all walls were filled with canned goods, food staples, and everything else you'd expect to find in a commissary.

We sat on the steps, maintaining dead silence. My friend handed me the rifle and whispered, "Hold this." A night-light barely provided enough light to see things. Just below the ceiling were steam pipes, water pipes, electrical wires, and other utility-type paraphernalia.

Suddenly, my friend nudged me in the side with his elbow and pointed to the steam pipe. A large rat, about the size of a squirrel, had emerged from atop the shelving in the corner of the room and was crawling slowly across the pipe.

My friend whispered, "Shoot him!" The rat paused as if he had heard something. I whispered, "I don't want to shoot him!" The rat began to move. My friend elbowed me forcefully and whispered with authority, "Shoot him!"

I raised the rifle, took aim, and fired. The explosion was deafening! The rat plummeted to the floor. We began to hear voices overhead. My friend said, "Let's get out of here!" We ran upstairs, out the back way, and returned to his room undetected.

We quickly undressed and got in bed. My friend giggled and whispered, "You sure are a good shot. I'm glad you didn't hit the pipe!" I said, "I didn't want to shoot the rat, anyway. I'll bet we're going to get in trouble!" He said, "Nobody will ever know it was us."

The next morning, when activity resumed in the cafeteria, someone spotted a spent 22-caliber shell casing and the remains of the rat. When he and I went down for breakfast, his mother confronted us. She grabbed my friend by the nape of the neck and asked sternly, "Did you shoot a rat in the basement last night?" He said, "No, ma'am!" Applying force to his neck, she said, "Don't you tell me a lie. We heard a shot last night. This morning we found an empty shell casing and a dead rat." He said, "I didn't shoot a rat last night. Eddie did!" Wow!

The lecture I got from his mother blew my appetite away! She was furious! She stated in emphatic terms, "If you can't behave better than that, you won't be allowed to come here anymore!"

As unpleasant as the experience was, I learned an important lesson – don't ever let anyone talk you into doing something you don't want to do.

SPIRITS-BREAD-DIDYAP

My father was a somewhat spirited man. He always seemed to be in high spirits. He frequently consumed some of the liquid-type spirits to influence his laissez-faire feeling of euphoria. This was during the days of prohibition. Alcoholic spirits were unlawful. People resorted to clandestine distilling and marketing of the product. The term to describe this activity was "bootlegging."

My father's source of corn during our years at Castle Pinckney was a little gray frame house on Cumberland Street not far from the Custom House. His bootlegger was a man named Henry. Henry used to dispense the goods in two-quart Mason jars. Occasionally, I was along when my father visited Henry. I came to know Henry and Henry came to know me.

Now that I had "come of age" in the rowing game, it fell to my lot to also become the rum-runner. On weekends, when the spirit supply would dwindle to the critical point, my father would give me a dollar bill. He would then tell me, "Go to Henry's and pick up a package." A "package" was a half gallon of moonshine (corn whiskey) in a Mason jar concealed in a brown paper bag.

I would get in the bateau, row across the harbor to the Engineer dock, walk to the Cumberland Street location and pick up the goods. Then, I would make the fearful trek back to the dock where I had left the bateau.

I was always terrified at the thought of getting caught in the illicit traffic of contraband booze. Holding the heavy paper bag in my arms, I felt exceedingly conspicuous. Anyone could readily tell that what I had in the bag was not a loaf of bread!

I would breathe a sigh of relief each time I safely reached the dock. I'd get in the bateau as quickly as I could and head for open water. Then, I would become beset with fear that the Coast Guard would apprehend me!

Each time I got safely back to Castle Pinckney after one of those missions, I felt as if I had evaded the "long arm of the law."

One Sunday morning about ten o'clock, my father and I rowed to the Standard Oil dock. He had to take care of some business. Meanwhile, I was to go to Cumberland Street, pick up a package, and meet him back at the dock.

As we were walking off the dock, we met Editor DidYap. There was a daily column running in *The News and Courier* at the time entitled, "Did You Happen to See?" In this column were items of general community interest written by a roving reporter who went about the city seeking incidents of appeal to share with the readers. The by-line nickname was "DidYap," a diminution of "Did You Happen."

My father knew the gentleman and stopped to chat with him. As he began his conversation, he turned to me, gave me a handful of money and said, "Go get a jar of corn and a loaf of bread. If you don't have enough money for both, don't get the bread."

I did as instructed. I had enough money, so I got both. The Standard Oil dock was a greater distance from

Cumberland Street than the Engineer dock. I trembled with fear as I returned to meet my father and head back home. "Another successful escape from the law," I thought as I strode onto the dock where he was waiting.

The next morning, in the "Did You Happen To See" column, this question appeared: "Did you happen to see a man at the Standard Oil dock giving his small son some money and telling him to go get a jar of 'corn' and a loaf of bread and, if he didn't have enough money for both, not to get the bread?"

Being probably the youngest rum-runner on the high seas at the time was bad enough! I certainly didn't want or need any publicity, especially with the likes of John Dillinger, Bonnie and Clyde, and "Baby Face" Nelson running loose!

Banner from column in *The News and Courier*, locals labeled as "DIDYAP." Picture courtesy of *The Post and Courier*.

Present day view of the Charleston skyline. Photo by Bill Smith.

The Ghosts of Castle Pinckney

Charleston skyline from Castle Pinckney around 1931. Photo courtesy of U.S. National Park Service.

Author's home on Castle Pinckney from the rear perimeter of lower yard. Photo courtesy of U.S. National Park Service.

I thought about all the good times we'd had together: skating, playing hide and seek, exploring, crabbing, riding the Dummy Line, catching fish, catching fiddlers, sleeping together in the double bed and everything else that came to mind concerning her.

A SAD SEA VOYAGE

The Corps of Engineers had a sea-going dredge named the *Comstock*. My father knew the captain and first mate very well and other members of the crew. Because I was with him from time to time in the activity around the Engineer dock, I also came to know many of the men with whom he worked or was acquainted.

Unbeknownst to me, my father had been talking with the first mate about Brownie, a German shepherd dog to which I was particularly endeared.

My father had purchased twenty-five little barred-rock biddies and brought them home to Castle Pinckney. He put them in a small wire enclosure in the backyard.

A day or two after he brought them home, old Brownie met me at the end of the dock when I arrived home from school. She always met and greeted me as if I were a member of some royal family. This day was different, however. Her tail wagged ever so slowly, her eyes were dull and blood shot, and I noticed welts all over her. She was in terrible distress and I knelt down beside her and began to hug and pet her.

She looked at me with those big, soft, brown eyes, in obvious distress and pain, and limped slowly up the dock as we walked together. I sensed something bad had taken place, but I couldn't imagine what.

As we arrived at the house, we met my father, who had a day off and was home. I inquired, "What happened to Brownie?" Without consideration, compassion, or sympathy, he said sternly, "We're getting rid of that dog and if you want to know what happened to her, I beat the devil out of her because she killed some of the biddies."

Again I knelt down beside her and began to hug and pet her, only this time the tears were streaming down my face and she was whimpering pathetically. "Crying won't do you any good," my father said, "my mind is made up." At that moment, I loved Brownie better than I loved my father.

After several days of intermittent weeping and grief, I resigned myself to the impending severance of a great relationship. Meanwhile, Brownie had begun to overcome the stress and ache of that horrible scourging. I thought to myself, "If dogs can think, I'll bet Brownie's thinking she doesn't want to live here anymore."

The next week, the *Comstock* was scheduled to go to Southport, North Carolina. The first mate lived there. He had already told my father that he would like to have the dog for his little children and that he would give her a really good home.

My father asked me, "How would you like to take an ocean trip on a sea-going dredge?" I replied, "I've never been to sea on a ship." He said, "The *Comstock* is going to Southport in a few days. The captain and the first mate said you'd be welcome to come along, if you like." I asked, "What about school?" He replied, "It won't hurt you to miss a day or two. It will be an experience to remember. You can ride back with the first mate. How about it?" Inspired by the opportunity to get out of school for a couple of days, I told him I would like to go.

The morning came for my first ocean trip on a large vessel. [Little did I ever dream that, one day, in an era called World War Two, I'd be flying Hellcat fighters from a carrier deck.] We were up early and all set for the trip. The boat to take us to Charleston was approaching. I was beginning to look forward to the trip with some degree of inflated anticipation when my father said, "Call Brownie and let's go!" Suddenly, I felt nauseated and wanted to renege, but we were beyond the point of no return. I tearfully did as instructed. The walk down the dock was the saddest experience of my life. I just couldn't bear the thought of giving up Brownie.

I was solemn and perturbed as we boarded the launch and headed for the Engineer dock where the *Comstock* was moored. I felt so sad and alone. Nobody cared. I was trapped, plumb helpless, in a snare of indescribable emotion. Brownie lay at my feet, oblivious to what was going on.

Once the launch reached the dock, my father, Brownie and I walked around to the slip where the *Comstock* was moored. My father exchanged greetings with everyone as we mounted the gangplank. Brownie walked very cautiously and close to me. The first mate met us and shook hands with my father, said, "Hi, there!" to me, then patted Brownie on the head and hugged her. He said, "Good girl! I know some little girls that are going to be thrilled to death." At that moment, I wished something would come and waft me away to somewhere out of this world. My heart was so heavy.

My father said, "Well, I guess I'd better be getting on to work. Have a good trip, son, and I'll see you when you get home." He expressed gratitude and appreciation to the first mate, then turned and headed for his office in the Custom House.

The first mate was really a very genuine man. He showed me and Brownie all about the ship. My father was right. I was beginning an "experience to remember." The mate took us to every nook and cranny, explaining the intricacies involved in the operation of a sea-going dredge – how it picked up sand and mud, stored it in the hold, and transported it to a dumping site. He showed us to our stateroom. He said, "You and Brownie can sleep in here." He then showed us the "head." I wondered where Brownie would go to the bathroom.

We cast off about noon, backed out of the berth, swung around and headed for the ocean. I saw the harbor and its surroundings from an entirely different perspective – the bridge of a large ship! We cruised slowly through the channel, past the East Bay area and South Battery. We followed the channel by Ripley and Fort Johnson, cruising out by Fort Sumter and Sullivan's Island. We entered the "Hallway to the World" as we passed between the jetties into the open sea.

The ocean was vast and magnificent. The winds were calm and there was a slow and shallow roll to the swells, just enough to give the ship an inkling of motion as it plied its course. Southport is due south of Wilmington, North Carolina, approximately 110 nautical miles northeast of Charleston.

Brownie was at my feet all the while.

She had to have some help on the ladders, but I didn't have to pick her up. By this time, she had made fast friends with the crew. They seemed delighted to have her on board. Actually, she claimed a lot more attention than I did.

Once we were through the jetties and on course, the bell rang. The mate asked if I were familiar with the ring. I shook my head. He said, "Chow time!" We went to the galley and had a scrumptious lunch. I was warming up to the experience in a big way. Losing Brownie was on the back burner, for the moment. As we ate, the mate said, "You can share some with her, if you want." It was just like home, feeding Brownie at the table.

All afternoon, we cruised across the briny. We passed several vessels, but mostly all we saw was water, water, water, and we were just looking at the top of it!

Around dusk, the bell rang, and we chowed down again. After we ate, the mate took me and Brownie to our "stateroom." I was grateful that he did; although he had shown it to me earlier, I had no idea where it was. I'd never have found that place in a million years!

The lights on a dredge are dim. I mean, *really* dim! I suppose there's no reason why they shouldn't be. A sea-going dredge is a utility vessel usually engaged in the traffic of mud. Mud just doesn't need bright lights. Also, the crew is limited, and all hands have multiple responsibilities.

Brownie and I laid down on the bunk. I lay on my side and tucked my knees toward my chin. She sprawled out at the foot of the bunk and snuggled up against my legs. I turned out the dim light and called it a day.

I lay there thinking about the activities of the day: how upset I was at the outset; how bitter I felt toward my father; the tour of the old dredge; the trip through the harbor; the stately, imposing city; the harbor surroundings, especially Castle Pinckney; Fort Johnson, Ripley, Fort Sumter, the jetties, and the ocean; the galley and feeding Brownie from the table on a ship. It all seemed like more than could happen in a single day.

As the ship rolled gently, my thoughts turned to Brownie. By this time, she was romping through the "Land of Nod." I reached down and put my hand on her head and left it there. She didn't move, secure in the comfort of my presence. I thought about all the good times we'd had together: skating, playing hide and seek, exploring, crabbing, riding the Dummy Line, catching fish, catching fiddlers, sleeping together in the double bed and everything else that came to mind concerning her. I thought resentfully about the whipping my father gave her.

"I won't see her anymore after tomorrow," I reminded myself. Then, I began to weep again. My hand was still resting on her head. I patted her several times and wept off to sleep.

Early the next morning, the sound of voices awakened me. The ship's motion had all but stopped. Brownie and I arose and headed for the deck. We had reached our destination. We were docking in Southport.

When the engines were shut down and the ship made secure, the mate came up to us. He said, "Did you sleep any?"

"Yessir," I answered. He patted Brownie on the head and said, "We're in Southport and all tied up. We can go ashore."

We made our way down the gangplank onto the dock and up to the parking area. As we strode along, I wondered about breakfast. I wanted to go to the galley again, but I didn't mention it. The crew probably had breakfast long before I even woke up.

We walked toward a car occupied by a lady and two little girls. The little girls got out and hurried to greet their daddy. Brownie had been close at my side all the while. When the kissing and hugging ended, the mate introduced me and we all exchanged greetings. He then stooped down and said, "And this is Brownie." A big lump came in my throat and my eyes welled up! The little girls put their arms around Brownie and began hugging her. She responded by wagging her tail. I could hardly stand it. Sensing my emotional distress, the mate's wife put her arm around my shoulder and said, "It's so wonderful of you to share your pet with us. Our children have always wanted a dog, and Brownie seems so gentle. They will love her to death."

I thought I would die! My eyes filled up again. I had to fight hard for constraint. We got into the car. Old Brownie and I sat in the back seat with the little girls. They were hugging and petting her and carrying on. She seemed to really like the attention.

In a few minutes, we pulled into the yard of their house. We stayed for an hour or so, during which time the lady, who was very nice, asked me if I'd had any breakfast. I said, "Not yet, but I'm really not hungry." She said, "Of course you're hungry, after being on the ocean all night." She prepared something for me to eat. While I was eating, the girls were getting better acquainted with Brownie.

Presently, the mate came in and said, "I suppose we'd better head on down to Charleston. It's a long drive." As I hugged Brownie for the last time, my eyes filled with tears of grief. I said goodbye to the lady and girls, then climbed into the car. The trip back was quiet, sad, and uneventful.

Once back home, I did my best to live with my grief. I was lost without my devoted companion. The one thing that made it bearable was the memory of the mate's wife putting a consoling arm around my shoulder and saying, "It's so wonderful of you to share your pet with us."

My dad was right. It really was an experience to remember!

Castle Pinckney

Once Backed As Home For Yankee Veterans

Castle Pinckney, that picturesque white elephant in Charleston harbor, was once enthusiastically backed by the Grand Army of the Republic as a site for a home for Yankee veterans of the Civil War.

The project was proposed by Abraham Charles Kaufman, a Charleston philanthropist, to a reunion of the Grand Army in Buffalo, N.Y., in 1897 and was unanimously approved by the veterans.

Mr. Kaufman proposed that the veterans' home be named for Maj. Robert Anderson, the federal commander of Fort Sumter at the outbreak of the Civil War.

Congress passed a bill appropriating money for the home but nothing ever came of the project.

Maj. J. C. Hemphill, editor of The News and Courier, com-

Do You Know Your Charleston?

mented on the project in the following language:

"Thanks to the splendid work of A. C. Kaufman, and the assistance of his Grand Army friends and the eloquence of the Rev. Dr. H. W. Bays, the project of establishing a sanitarium for the veterans, soldiers and sailors in Charleston harbor was unanimously, endorsed by the Grand Army of the Republic at Buffalo, N.Y., yesterday. The scene in the encampment at the conclusion of Dr. Bays' address and when the question was submitted to the old soldiers must have been thrilling, and we can well imagine that Mr. Kaufman was well-nigh overcome by the brilliant success of his unselfish and patriotic endeavors."

Built on an island known as Shute's Folly Island, Castle Pinckney was first constructed as a fort for use during the War of 1812 but saw no action.

In the Civil War, it was main-tained as a harbor fort but saw use only briefly as a prison for a few federal prisoners.

It was used sporadically over the century since the Civil War by federal agencies including the Coast Guard and the Army's Corp of Engineers.

In 1958 the S.C. Ports Authority obtained title to the land and began a drive to restore the fort as an historic tourist attraction. The drive fizzled in 1962 due to lack of funds.

Since then Castle Pinckney has nestled quietly off the Battery often mistaken by tourists for its more famous sister, Fort Sumter.

CASTLE PINCKNEY WAS OLD HARBOR FORT
A 'White Elephant' in Charleston Harbor often mistaken by tourists as Fort Sumter. (Staff Photo flown by Carolina Skyways).

Over the years, many proposals have been made concerning the fate of Castle Pinckney. This idea appeared in *The News and Courier* on June 15, 1964. Courtesy of *The Post and Courier*.

Bingo! The hook slipped in the sling, the bow of the boat shot up like a homesick angel, the stern went plummeting in the opposite direction, and I sailed into space and landed in the water in some twisted contortion as I attempted to create a "diving" posture.

LAUNCHING THE NEWLY PAINTED BATEAU

We had one special unit of transportation at Castle Pinckney. Today, it would probably be described as a wooden "jon boat"; back then, it was "King of Bateaux."

Made of select, knot-free cypress, it was twelve feet long with a forty-two-inch beam. It tapered to a sixteen-inch bow and a twenty-six-inch stern. The bow piece and the transom were made of oak. The deck was one-by-six cypress boards positioned perpendicular to the sides. There was one seat just aft of center, one in the stern and a small seat up in the bow that just fit me. When we were gigging, the battery occupied this seat. The boat had galvanized oar-lock holders and oar-locks. A pair of six-foot oars were the standard propulsion.

We also had a unique propulsion mechanism called an "Elto." The Elto is my earliest recollection of an outboard motor. This little unit was a real gem. It had a self-contained gas tank on the top where the flywheel was. It had a little two-bladed propeller and an aluminum rudder to which were attached very small ropes for directional control. On the flywheel was a spring-loaded knob for cranking.

When we first acquired the Elto, I wasn't strong enough to crank it. It didn't take me long, however, to develop sufficient cranking power to make it hum.

Most of the time, we used the oars. They were best for cruising around the island and up the creek. We used the bateau to crab in, fish in, gig in, explore the marsh in, and play in. It was also our main link with Charleston when the Engineer dock was closed, such as non-working hours, on weekends, and holidays. When it became necessary to go to the city during those times, the little Elto was set in place on the transom and putt, putt, putt we'd go, gliding across the harbor.

Charleston harbor is a marvelous expanse of shimmering water. What a view we had from Castle Pinckney! It was a panorama of history. When we first arrived, we were exceedingly intrigued by the surrounding beauty. From the porch of our house, which faced the city, we could observe James Island, the Ashley River, South Battery, and all the buildings on East Bay Street, including the docks. In the background, standing tall in spiritual splendor, loomed the spires of the ancient churches, especially St. Michael's. Beside the city, the Cooper and Wando rivers branched out to wind their way through the interior of the lower part of our state.

When the Grace Memorial Bridge was completed, it added decoration of unimaginable magnitude and grandeur. Its giant spans graced the skyline over the apex of the Cooper and Wando rivers. It hung there, suspended in majesty, like exquisite tapestry from some ancient Corinthian order.

From the back hemisphere of the island, we looked out at: Ripley, a channel marker and lighthouse, long since extinct; Fort Johnson, where the quarantine station was located; Morris Island, where we used to go by bateau to gather sea shells; Fort Sumter, which rises in formidable prominence at the entrance to the harbor; the jetties, with their massive rocks in a row, controlling the shifting sands as they maintain a channel for ships entering the timeless harbor; Sullivan's Island; Shem Creek; and Mount Pleasant.

Sometimes, the water was not conducive to navigation in the bateau. If the wind was blowing strong enough to disturb the water to any degree of turmoil, being out there in a bateau was something less than safe. Strong tidal currents also had an adverse affect if one were going in the opposite direction. When we plied the harbor in the bateau, we were always careful to plan our trips to coincide with favorable tidal movement.

I recall an occasion when I was rowing to Charleston to meet my father. He was going to Columbia to do some inspection work at the Saluda Dam project and was taking me along with him. That morning, when I left home, the tide was in the waning hours of the ebb and was racing out to sea something fierce.

I recall the severe struggle of that trip with vivid discomfort. Each time I would dip the oar blades in the water and pull through a stroke, the bateau would glide forward about six feet. As I raised the oars to begin another stroke, the current would push me back about three feet. I had to accelerate my strokes to a degree of taxing rapidity. After what seemed like hours of extreme exertion, I pulled into the Standard Oil dock, exhausted beyond belief and my arms and back in knots. I'll never be convinced that that trip to Saluda Dam was worth all the suspense and agony.

When the time came to paint the bateau, my father pulled it out of the water, scraped and sanded the cypress, tightened the brass screws holding the small craft together, and readied her in all manner for a new coat of paint. His favorite color was battleship grey. He was influenced, I suppose, by the Naval vessels that frequently moved in and out of the harbor with their air of superiority. Sometimes, they would moor for days right in our front yard.

Painting was the final step in the overhaul. My father took great pains to ensure that every stroke of the brush did its job well. When he had finished, the little boat looked like new money!

The day for launching arrived. We put the bateau on the Dummy Line and rolled it to the end of the wharf where the loading ramp was. On a platform to the left side of the loading ramp, there was a large derrick used for loading and unloading heavy objects transported by boat.

My father decided to use the derrick to launch the boat. He also decided to launch with the Elto in place. This made the stern outweigh the bow, so it would be necessary to have some ballast on board to give the boat balance. Guess what was chosen to be ballast! You got it! I was!

Fashioning a sling of rope, my father secured one end in a loop around the bow and the other in a loop around the stern. He went over to the derrick and maneuvered the boom so that the cable with the big hook on it would swing in place over the sling. He then placed the sling in the hook using a small loop. Everything was all set. He said, "Hop in." I jumped into the bateau as he started the engine on the derrick. I was squatting in the bottom of the bateau, just forward of the middle seat, as he had instructed me, to balance the weight. He slowly began the elevation process to lift the boat from the Dummy Line. As the boat lifted off of the flat bed and swung into the air, a sensation of grandeur came over me. I felt as if I were on a magic carpet in some oriental paradise heading for the city Four Square and streets of pure gold.

My father swung the boom out over the water at the end of the dock. Man, this was magnificent! I was in an air boat! Yahoo!! I looked down at the water and wished I hadn't. It was a long way between where I was and where it was. My father began to lower the boat slowly toward the water. Bingo! The hook slipped in the sling, the bow of the boat shot up like a homesick angel, the stern went plummeting in the opposite direction, and I sailed into space and landed in the water in some twisted contortion as I attempted to create a "diving" posture. As

I smacked into the water, "smarts" began stinging my body.

When I surfaced, I looked up at the dock. My father was standing at the edge of the wharf, convulsing with laughter, looking down at me. I failed to see the humor. It's a wonder I didn't break my neck!

I swam around to the ladder and climbed back up onto the dock unharmed, but really shaken up.

My father now decided to haul in the bateau, place it back on the Dummy Line, and roll it to the landing steps at the water's edge. He removed the motor and pulled the boat down the stairs into the water. The procedure was so simple and effective. The boat slid into the water with much more grace than I demonstrated in the previous launch attempt.

I thought to myself, "Why didn't you do that in the first place instead of making me the *man on the flying TRAP-eze*?"

Equipment used by the Army Corps of Engineers and others were often stored at Castle Pinckney. Photo courtesy of U.S. National Park Service.

73

"TALL BETSY"

The Corps of Engineers kept a night watchman stationed at Castle Pinckney to protect the interests of the War Department. He lived in an area of the office building where an efficiency apartment had been arranged for him.

This gentleman, of African descent, was one of the greatest personalities I ever encountered. His formal education was practically nonexistent. He gained his knowledge from experience and exposure to the rigors of the "college of hard knocks."

He was warm, affectionate, kind, considerate, and understanding. His manners were impeccable. We soon considered ourselves related to him.

Each payday, he would remember us children by bringing a small paper bag full of what he called "jawbone breakers," a very hard, round, sweet-flavored candy. Were the candy unavailable, he would substitute Johnny Cakes, a large style of sugar cookies about three inches in diameter. We always looked forward to and appreciated his treats. His generosity and kind disposition endeared him to our hearts forever.

When we moved to Castle Pinckney, the night watchman surveillance was rescheduled for weeknights only.

There were several punch-clock stations strategically placed about the island. Nightly, he would make his scheduled rounds. He always hummed as he went about his chores. Not just a normal or low-decibel hum, but an exaggerated one, as if broadcasting his presence to frighten away would-be harm-bearing critters lurking in the darkness.

We also had a live-in domestic lady of African descent. She performed household chores and did most of the cooking. Like the night watchman, she worked weekdays. She was a great cook and knew just how to enhance flavor in food with her technique and expertise.

She was not as warm, jovial, and personable as the night watchman, but we loved her just as much. Her personality didn't really respond very readily to three rambunctious children who always seemed to be in her way.

During the daytime hours, the kitchen was a most popular place. We were constantly looking for something to eat or something to drink, or both.

She was quite the disciplinarian and we children derived immeasurable benefit from her presence. She taught us how to "be respectful" and how to "mind." She admonished us in the ways of cleanliness and frequently reminded us to mind our manners.

She and the night watchman were an odd combination, with personalities a hundred and eighty degrees out of phase. Each night after our family had finished dining, she would prepare her plate and one for the night watchman. They would sit at the table in the dim lamplight, eat and talk, laugh and argue. Sometimes, the arguments would heat up enough to cause concern. There were times when we thought they were at each other's throat.

We "devilish young'uns" used to linger on the porch outside the kitchen and eavesdrop. We would stifle laughter until we couldn't hold it anymore, then burst out hilariously. She would come running out and get after us with some choice words of admonition.

We had a large pantry connected to the kitchen. A common wall separated the bathroom and the pantry. Our domestic lady slept in the pantry. She shared all other facilities. Opposite the entrance door from the kitchen to the pantry was a large window. Except in cold weather, the window was always open.

One summer evening, when the domestic lady and the night watchman had finished their supper and were sitting at the table exchanging barbs, we children decided to stage some disruptive antics.

We got the broom, a white pillow case, a coat hanger, an old, straw sun hat, and an old, full-length coat. We pulled the pillow case over the straw end of the broom. With crayons, we sketched a very grotesque face on the pillow case. It looked really hideous. We then hooked the coat hanger in the broom straw and made it secure. Next, we placed the old coat on the hanger and held up the broom. We all began laughing. We had created a "Tall Betsy." My sister raised it up and, holding onto the broomstick, pulled the coat around her. I buttoned the coat. She was obscured, but could peep through the area between the buttons. What an awesome creation! The last adornment was one of our mother's large, wide-brimmed, straw sun hats. We neatly tied it on top of the head of the Betsy.

We had fashioned an image that took on exaggerated proportions of real life. It was the spookiest thing we had ever seen. Then, the fun began!

We stealthily marched single-file from the bedroom down the hall, across the porch, to the kitchen door. The night watchman was sitting at the table. The domestic lady had a plate of fried fish in her hand and was about to place it in the cupboard.

My sister lowered the Tall Betsy enough to get it through the kitchen door, then raised it up. Not a word was said. The Tall Betsy spoke for herself. In the dim light of the kerosene lamp, the night watchman, with a fear-stricken expression, stammered, "Eh, eh! Eh, eh! Who dat?" He spontaneously bolted from the table toward the pantry door, the only avenue of escape. The domestic lady simultaneously looked, screamed to the top of her lungs, and also streaked for the pantry door. We can't describe what took place after they jammed together in the pantry door on their way to escape through the pantry window. We do know that the window screen was demolished and fried fish was scattered all over the yard. Fortunately, no one was injured.

Humor is always at someone's expense! We children laughed and laughed. Our mother and father heard the commotion and came running from the living room. They immediately read the scene. Then, discretion being the better part of valor, they rebuked us for frightening the people.

My father went out in the yard and called the watchman and the domestic lady back inside. He explained to them that ours was just a childish prank and no harm was meant. He smoothed over the ruffled feathers and they condescended not to murder us kids.

The Ghosts of Castle Pinckney

We knew from our experiences with them that they were superstitious, and the introduction of the Tall Betsy created a never-to-be-forgotten farce. The night watchman and the domestic lady eventually came to remember it with a sense of humor. We laughed about it many times together.

We have remembered our prank through the years, the dimension of which spooked two people right through a window screen and demolished a plate of tasty fish. To this day, the recollection provokes much laughter.

It's a good thing the window wasn't too high off the ground.

Left rear side of the old fort wall. Photo by Bill Smith.

The regal bird, in all his pomp and splendor, would sit perched on top of the pole until time came to go fishing. Then, he would lift off with awe-inspiring natural grace and beauty.

A BALD EAGLE'S PERCH

Castle Pinckney was, without doubt, the most ideal place in the world for a preteen boy to grow up. The other stories in this collection attest to the variety of experiences that support this premise.

This story about the Bald Eagle is a special chapter in the book of life at Castle Pinckney. It is a thrilling episode of daily observations, where, as a boy, I delighted in coastal nature at its zenith.

Where else on earth could a young lad, seven through twelve years of age, pack so much life into the opportunities presented each day? I lived every moment to the fullest. I learned to love nature in its finest and most spectacular hours.

The bald eagle! A diurnal bird of prey, it frequented the marsh and waters of Castle Pinckney.

A very large, painted sign signaled the presence of underwater telephone cables that serviced the office at Castle Pinckney. The stately sign stood in the tip of the marsh on the Charleston end of the island and boldly advised all who passed, "CABLE CROSSING. DO NOT ANCHOR."

Near the sign was an abandoned pole, perhaps from another era of channel warnings. This pole was far from being just another pole. This pole had personality and significance. It was the favorite lookout post of a large bald eagle that frequented the island as if it were his own private, secluded habitat.

The regal bird, in all his pomp and splendor, would sit perched on top of the pole until time came to go fishing. Then, he would lift off with awe-inspiring natural grace and beauty. After losing a little altitude as he gained momentum, he would then soar out over the cool, clear waters of Charleston harbor.

The eagle would glide up, down and around, cruising the area until he spotted his quarry. Once "eagle eye" homed in, he would swoop down to the water. Almost effortlessly, with remarkable timing, his talons would abruptly penetrate the surface as he snatched a fish from the depths.

He would return to his perch and partake of the spoils. You could see his head raise and lower as he clutched the fish and fragmented the flesh into bite-sized morsels.

Even now, it seems as though I can hear my father's voice. Early in the morning, after noticing the pole occupied, he would emphatically call out, "Bald eagle's on his perch!"

This became a frequent and memorable expression. The first family member to notice the emblem bird would cry out, "Bald eagle's on his perch!" All others would move toward a window or step out on the porch to verify the announcement and watch for the eagle to make a move.

The bald eagle was a part of the heritage of Castle Pinckney. Today, folks would say, "He went with the territory." He possessed and demonstrated a distinct air of superiority. With his distinguished, gleaming, snow-white head, he gave all the appearance of a sophisticated "Solon of the Seashore."

On days when the eagle was not observed soaring or perched, we were exceedingly apprehensive. We always pondered the possibility that some ill fate may have befallen him.

Many times, after we had concluded that some heartless gun-wielder "had done him in for the sport of it," the eagle would appear from nowhere and, to our delight, take his place on his perch.

My father particularly enjoyed the presence of the eagle. He taught me to admire and respect the great bird. He explained the nature, personality and characteristics of the "monarch of the sky." He emphasized the eagle's lofty position, having been chosen as the official national emblem for our country. He admonished me, "Don't ever kill an eagle, bald or otherwise!"

The most thrilling act in the bald eagle's repertoire took place when the osprey would invade his territory looking for a fish. Old Bald would sit still on his perch and observe. When the fish hawk would move in on a fish and rise out over the water with his prey, the gallant, domineering king of birds would move in on the fish hawk. After a split-second, midair encounter, the eagle would leave the scene with fish-in-talon while the osprey went back to fishing. Returning to his perch, the eagle would enjoy the spoils of the raid.

The "CABLE CROSSING. DO NOT ANCHOR" sign and the eagle's pole have vanished. The eagle, too, has long since abandoned the territory and "given up the ghost."

Each time I glance out across the harbor and fix my eyes on the tip of the island, I get a mental image. In my mind's eye, I can see Old Bald sitting on the pole, and I can hear "Bald eagle's on his perch!" echoing through the halls of memory of Castle Pinckney.

An 1861 photo of the barracks, guards above, prisoners below.

Battery emplacements atop the fort on Castle Pinckney in 1865, after the fall of Charleston.

It was nearly midnight when we went to bed. We drifted off into the "Land of Nod," thinking about what was to have been a spectacular fireworks display and how it turned into an exciting, but sobering, rescue.

FIREWORKS

One winter, the city of Charleston was staging a fireworks extravaganza in celebration of the Christmas season. A huge barge was anchored in the harbor, positioned just off East Battery. The fireworks spectacular was scheduled to begin when darkness settled in.

Our family anxiously awaited the event. We had watched all the preparation, beginning with the towing of the barge to the anchoring site. All of Charleston was humming with activity, anticipation, and expectation.

For several days, the preparations progressed. We could see the boats taking the necessary paraphernalia from the docks to the barge. We could see the men as they worked on the deck of the barge making everything ready. Significant emphasis was placed on safety. Special precautions were taken to prevent any kind of disaster.

The anticipation increased daily as the countdown progressed. All afternoon on the scheduled date, people from throughout the low country gathered on the Battery and other spots of unobstructed observation. We were dancing and cavorting on the front porch, imagining the same was taking place in the streets of Old Charleston.

At Castle Pinckney, we had the best seats in the house for the event. No crowds or noise. Just our family. From the privacy of our loge, we could really enjoy the show.

Finally, the hour arrived. Five... four... three... two... one... detonation! The show had begun. There was an enormous explosion and the night momentarily turned to day. Then, all became silent as darkness enveloped the scene. What happened? What is going on? Questions, questions, but no answers. It was apparent, however, that, with the explosion, the display had come to an abrupt, premature, untimely demise.

After about an hour of patience and conjecture, we concluded it was all over. We were very disappointed. We were sad that it ended that way after all the time, energy, effort, and excitement invested in its planning, promotion, and preparation.

As we were talking, my father suddenly said, "Hush, I think I heard someone calling." We mummed up. A distant, anguished cry of "Help!" drifted through the air. We listened intently. "Help!" seemingly a little closer. It was very dark. Visibility was nil. "Help me!" louder and more distinct.

The voice was coming from the marsh area facing Charleston. My father called back, "We're here. We can help." The voice kept crying out, "Help! Help me!" and kept coming closer. My father went down to the yard on the lower level. The person calling approached the rock-bound edge of the yard. My father called in response, "We're here, come this way. Be careful of the large rocks. They have barnacles and oyster shells on them."

A man, invisible because of the darkness, came to the edge of the rocks. My father took him by the arm to help him over the rocks. The man kept crying, "Help! Help me!" My father tried to console him, saying, "It's okay, now. You're safe. We can help you." "Help! Help me!" the man pleaded.

My father helped the man to the upper level and led him into the kitchen where the lamp was burning. We had an Aladdin lamp with a mantle, so the room was well lit.

The sight of the man was horrible. He was soaking wet, muddy, battered, bleeding, and shocked out of his mind. "Help, help me," he kept saying. My father led him to a seat and directed my mother to get some blankets and some of my clothes. He continued to console the man as he washed the blood away from his blackened face. He washed the cuts and bruises on his arms and legs. My mother brought the blankets and the clothes. My father told us kids to go out on the porch. We did.

Father removed the man's wet clothing, examined him, bathed him and dried him off. There were numerous obvious cuts and bruises. My father cleaned him up well enough to determine that there was no serious trauma. Using the clothes my mother had brought in, he got the stranger dressed. My father's clothes fit the man rather well. Father wrapped a blanket around the man and gave him some black coffee. Dazed, trembling and moaning, he drank the coffee. "Help! Help me!" he cried again. My father gave him a shot of white lightning. In a little while, the man began to calm down, so it must have helped. He slowly became more rational.

Still trembling and bleeding, he related the story. He had been on the barge when it exploded. He was literally stunned and blown overboard. Coming to his senses in the water, dazed, distraught and disoriented, he began to swim. He swam and swam, not knowing in which direction he was going or if it would lead to anywhere. He unintentionally came ashore in the marsh and oyster beds of Castle Pinckney, though he knew not where he was.

Although still dazed and disoriented as he came ashore, he had recovered enough to observe the light from our kitchen. He began to move toward our house, crying for help.

"Now that I'm safe, I feel better," he said. My father continued talking with him, wiping away fresh blood and trying to console him. He seemed to be recovering. Another shot of white lightning and more black coffee were offered.

Presently, he began to regain composure. It had been about an hour since he stumbled ashore at Castle Pinckney. My father said to him, "I'll take you to Charleston where you can see a doctor and get in touch with your family. Do you think you can ride in a bateau?" He indicated he could, expressed his appreciation to my father, mother, and us kids (all we did was gawk!), and left with my father to return to the city.

It was nearly midnight when we went to bed. We drifted off into the "Land of Nod," thinking about what was to have been a spectacular fireworks display and how it turned into an exciting, but sobering, rescue.

Smoke and flame, whipped by stiff wind, rise from building on Castle Pinckney. (Staff Photo by Swain)

Castle Pinckney Building Is Destroyed By Flames

POST 12/23/67

A frame building atop the old fortification at Castle Pinckney in Charleston harbor was destroyed by a spectacular fire yesterday.

Hundreds of spectators lined the Battery to watch the blaze, which was fanned by 30-mile-an-hour winds.

While the ruins smoldered for hours afterwards, the blaze took very little time to complete its destructive work.

The cause of the fire has not been determined and will likely remain that way, since Castle Pinckney is outside of the city limits and the Charleston Fire Department's jurisdiction and a Coast Guard spokesman said they have no one qualified to determine the cause.

THE BLAZE was battled by units of the city fire department, the Coast Guard and tugs from White Stack Towing Company, but there was never much hope of saving the wooden structure.

The fire department got the first call about 4 p.m. and notified the Coast Guard. The Coast Guard requested and got a detail of men from the department, but by the time they arrived on the island there was little they could do but prevent the fire from spreading to the

Here's how Castle Pinckney looked before the fire.

The December 22, 1967 fire which destroyed all the buildings on Castle Pinckney, as reported by *The News and Courier*. Courtesy of *The Post and Courier*.

I was looking eye-to-eye at the largest rattlesnake I had ever seen, and the head was drawn back in an "S," as if to strike. Then, I came to the fullest understanding of the term "petrified"! Even so, I dropped the rabbit and leaped for my life.

RATTLESNAKE!

In the summer of 1935, we moved from Castle Pinckney to Saint Andrews Parish, west of the Ashley, leaving behind forever the six-year saga of residential bliss.

All was not entirely peaceful, however. A serious fracture had occurred in the marital relationship of my mother and father. The gap widened and the union succumbed to divorce. When this occurred, my mother took my older sister and moved to Savannah, Georgia. My younger sister and I stayed with our father. We lived in a little cabin he had built on six acres of property not far from the Maryville community. Our lifestyle made a dramatic change. My younger sister and I became like waifs as we struggled together for survival.

We were all but abandoned, seldom seeing our father and virtually fending for ourselves. We were successful in making friends with the family living nearest us. Their house was about a hundred yards away. I feel certain that sympathy sponsored the friendship more than anything else, but the lady who lived there was an angel.

We also made friends with a family that lived about half a mile further down the road. This family of less-than-modest means consisted of seven persons – a father, a mother, three sons, a daughter and a paternal grandfather. The children were in our age range and attended school with us. We all became pals.

The area where we lived was strictly rural, but was developing into more of a suburban community as Charleston expanded. West of the Ashley was an optional direction.

Once, I hiked with the three boys from the family down the road to Legare Island to spend the night. Legare Island was a focal point for the Boy Scouts of America troops in Charleston. This site was the destination for the seven-mile hike necessary for completing certain Merit Badge requirements. We lived about four miles from Legare Island.

We packed some bread and peanut butter, a short supply of water, a candle, a blanket each and headed for the island about midafternoon.

The weather was bright and balmy. The woods were still, fresh, and aromatic as we strolled down the little-used, two-rut road. Sand in the ruts was bleached white and quite warm to our feet. The grass in the center lane was tall, green and seedy. The roadsides were ditched, but had become overgrown with foliage.

The four of us ambled along, talking, laughing, having a wonderful time in the woods. We commented about the different birds we saw and argued about some we couldn't identify. We were fascinated by deer tracks and other signs of animal life.

The last leg of the approach to Legare Island was mud, and, by the time we reached the island, what we needed most was a bath. It was now late in the afternoon. We explored the island and saw evidence of other camping activity, but nothing really exciting. The old hut on the island was in quite a state of dilapidation. Windows were broken out, the door sagged on the jamb, and bricks were loose in the fire place. The floor was unswept and very dirty. It looked like a long time had passed since anyone had used the cabin.

Dusk was closing in on us, so we lit the candle. We had peanut butter sandwiches by candlelight and consumed all our water. We talked and joked and carried on like kids usually do. Now, it was dark. The lone flicker of the candle struggled, but produced only very dim illumination. The candle was just a short section of what it used to be and we knew it would not survive the night. We began to wonder if we would.

None of us had a watch, so we forgot time. We became beset with anxiety. When we'd stop talking, all we would hear were mysterious night sounds. We talked loud and long, each one trying to conceal the degree of his fear. We decided to spread our blankets and try to get some sleep. There was more loud talk and giggling.

Ever since sunset, the air had been heavy with the hum of mosquitoes. We'd been battling them all night. When we laid down on the dirty floor, the mosquitoes stepped up their siege. The warm air discounted the need for cover, but protection from the mosquitoes demanded it. The misery of that night was incredible. Sleep was impossible, the mosquitoes assaulted us unmercifully, and we tossed all over the floor. The night dragged on after the candle burned out. Four kids, and each one too brave to admit it, but all wishing they were home. Whose idea was this, anyway?

At the first hint of dawn, we were already plodding off the island, mosquito-bitten, tired, hungry, and thirsty.

We were quiet and uncomfortable as we trekked homeward. The sun was brightening up the day. The woods were beautiful but had lost the attraction and appeal of the day before. The mood was somber. Each of us was engulfed in personal misery.

As we rounded a bend in the two-rut road, I was walking some distance ahead of the other three. Suddenly, I noticed a little rabbit jumping up and down, cutting flips, apparently in some distress. I quickly ran to where it was, knelt down, and picked it up. At that instant, I heard the most blood-curdling, unnerving hiss of my life, followed almost simultaneously by a most distinct and petrifying high-pitched rattle. I froze, held my breath, and glanced toward the sound. I was looking eye-to-eye at the largest rattlesnake I had ever seen, and the head was drawn back in an "S," as if to strike. Then, I came to the fullest understanding of the term "petrified"! Even so, I dropped the rabbit and leaped for my life.

The others had rounded the bend and saw me moving out. They yelled, "What's the matter?" I yelled, "Rattlesnake!" They came tearing down the far side of the road opposite where the rabbit lay, passed the spot and hastened to join me. I was trembling, breathless, and white as a sheet.

We ran and trotted the rest of the way home, a distance of about a mile and a half.

As providence would have it, just as we reached our house, my father arrived home. We related the story to him. He said, "Get in the car. We'll go see if the snake is still there." He picked up a large burlap bag and a five-gallon can with a lid on it. We piled in the car and drove back to the snake site.

He stopped the car just short of where the rabbit had fallen, and walked to the spot. My father searched cautiously for the snake. We followed. He suddenly raised his hand in a "stop" motion and said, "Here he is, and he has swallowed the rabbit." He backed up to where we kids were standing and said, "I'll cut a forked stick and we'll capture that rascal."

He looked around in the bushes until he spied a suitable snake prong. Using his pocket knife, he cut the branch. It was about four feet long and had a wide "V" on the end. He said, "Let's go back and see what we can do. You boys don't get too close."

We returned to the spot. We boys couldn't see the snake, but my father did. He slowly maneuvered the prong into place, then quickly pressed it down on the snake, just behind his head. Holding pressure on the stick, he reached down and grabbed the snake behind the head and raised him up. Boy, was that snake bad and mad! He writhed, wriggled, twisted and wrapped his shiny gleaming, diamond-back body around my father's arm. My father called, "Get me the bag and can!" I brought them to him. He slipped the burlap bag over the snake, tied it off and dropped bag and snake into the can and closed the lid.

"Guess where we're going now," he said as we returned to the car. I asked, "Where?" "There is only one place for this big snake and that's the museum," he said. We drove to the Charleston Museum on Rutledge Avenue. Upon arrival, we thirsty boys paused for a long, cool drink from the old flowing well before going in with our donation.

The curator was happy to get such a fine specimen. He measured the big snake. It was four and a half feet long. It brandished eight rattles and a "button."

The curator placed the snake in a "live exhibit" glass case for all to see. The next day, *The News and Courier* carried the story. We boys thought we had arrived!

High-tide view of Castle Pinckney and the beautiful harbor waters. Photo courtesy of U.S. National Park Service.

Birds'-eye view of Charleston Harbor and environs, *Harper's Weekly*, August 15, 1861, taken from an issue of *Harper's Weekly*, 1961. Picture courtesy of Special Collections–College of Charleston.

The Ghosts of Castle Pinckney

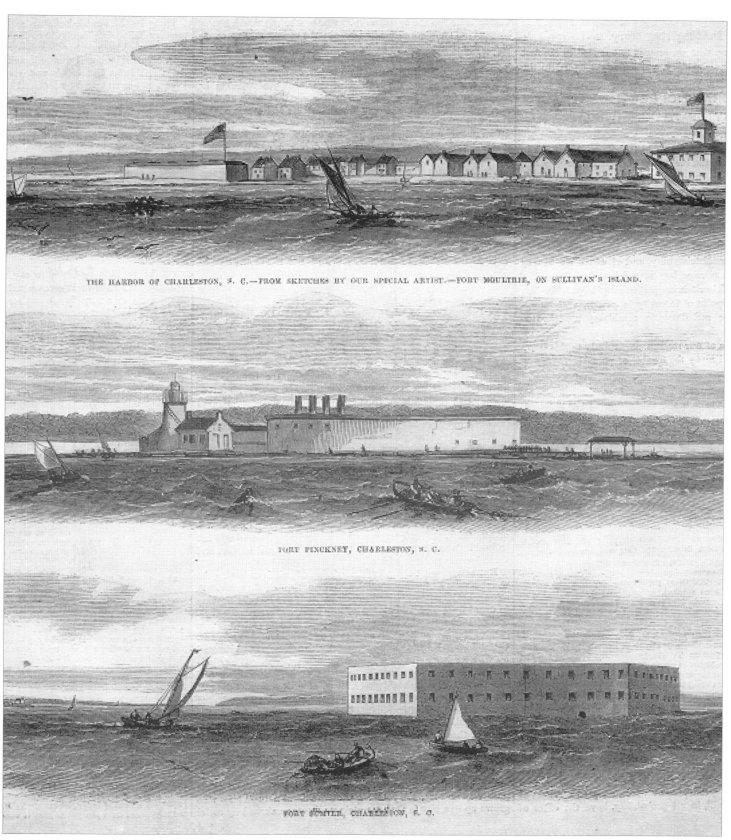

THE HARBOR OF CHARLESTON, S. C.—FROM SKETCHES BY OUR SPECIAL ARTIST.—FORT MOULTRIE, ON SULLIVAN'S ISLAND.

FORT PINCKNEY, CHARLESTON, S. C.

FORT SUMTER, CHARLESTON, S. C.

Engravings of Fort Moultrie, Fort Pinckney and Fort Sumter as they appeared in *Frank Leslie's Illustrated Newspaper*, April 27, 1860. Picture courtesy of Special Collections–College of Charleston.

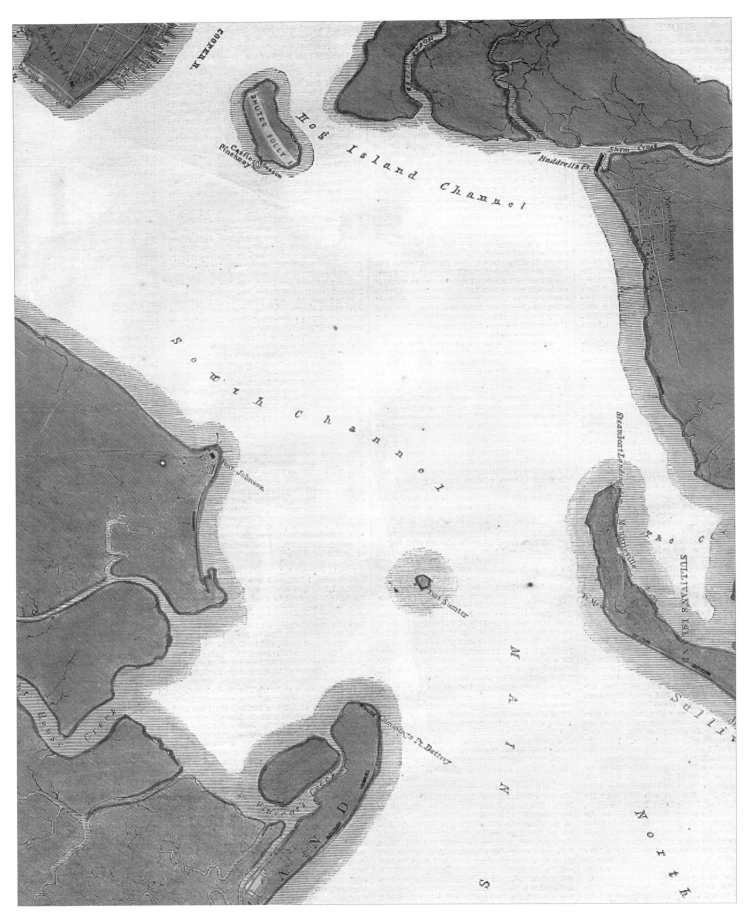

Map of Charleston Harbor as it appeared in *Harper's Weekly*, April 27,1861. Picture courtesy of Special Collections–College of Charleston.

The Ghosts of Castle Pinckney

"Buzz" McClellan holding Susan Collins, his 2nd cousin, in 1934.

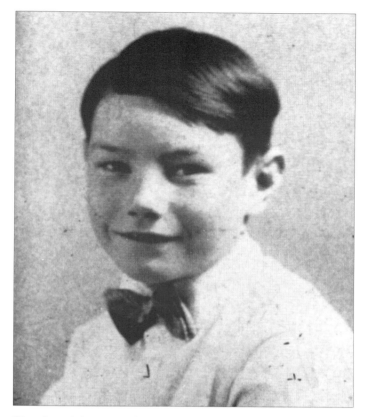

"Buzz" at eight years of age.

The Castle Pinckney kids on an outing to Morris Island around 1931. Left to right: "Buzz," older sister Leila Ruth, and younger sister Esther Carolyn.

Author's older sister, Leila Ruth, at age 9.

"Buzz," seated in goat cart, and friend Simons Hasel enjoy a ride. Simons was killed in 1934 as a teenager in a shooting mishap.

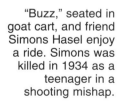

Author's younger sister, Esther Carolyn, at age 4.

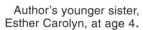

E. P. McClellan, Jr.

Author's sons (L-R) Barry Lynn McClellan, Brian Thomas McClellan and Christopher Palmer McClellan.

Author's grandchildren Robert Edward and Kelley Jean McClellan.

Author's grandchildren Joshua Aaron and Rachel Elizabeth McClellan.

Author's grandchildren Orion Palmer, Melanie Jane and Jacob Ezra McClellan.

Author's grandson Matthew George McClellan strikes pose reminiscent of illustration of Buzz in "Rats!" story (page 58).

The Ghosts of Castle Pinckney

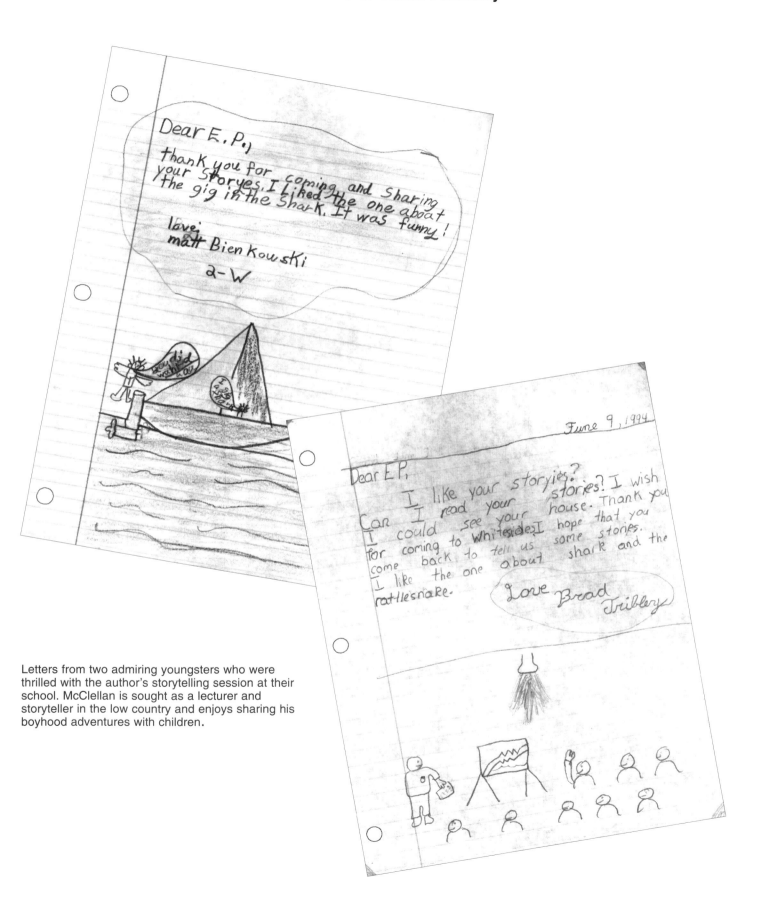

Dear E. P.,

thank you for coming and sharing your storyes. I liked the one about the gig in the shark. It was funny!

love,
matt Bienkowski
2-W

June 9, 1994

Dear E.P.,

I like your storyies? Can I read your stories? I wish I could see your house. Thank you for coming to Whiteside. I hope that you come back to tell us some stories. I like the one about shark and the rattlesnake.

Love Brad Tribley

Letters from two admiring youngsters who were thrilled with the author's storytelling session at their school. McClellan is sought as a lecturer and storyteller in the low country and enjoys sharing his boyhood adventures with children.

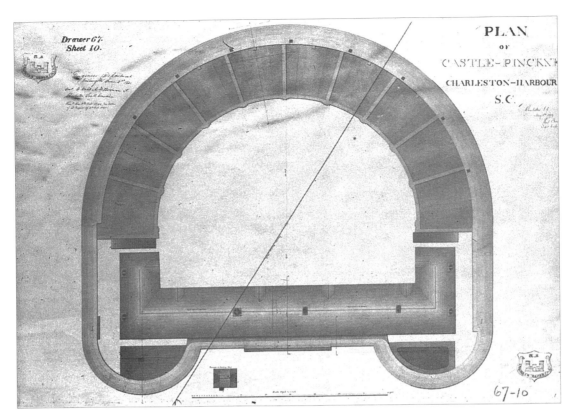

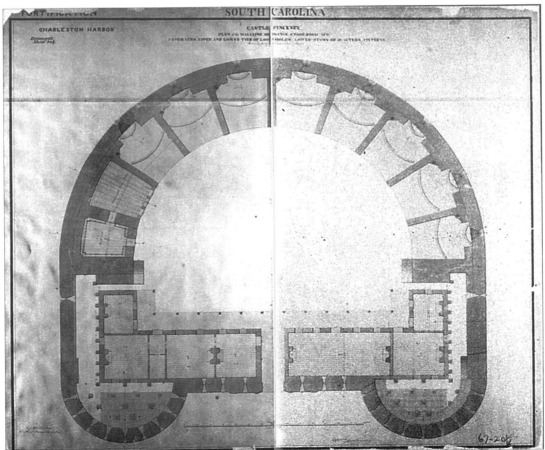

Top: roof level of castle and buildings. Bottom: ground level of castle and buildings.

The Ghosts of Castle Pinckney

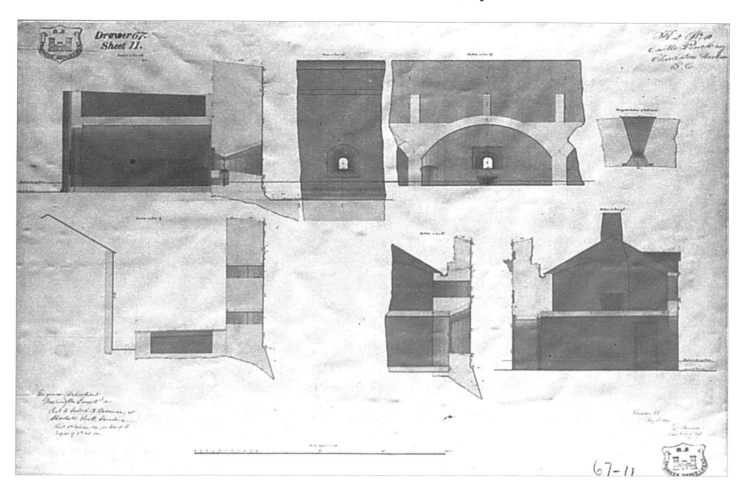

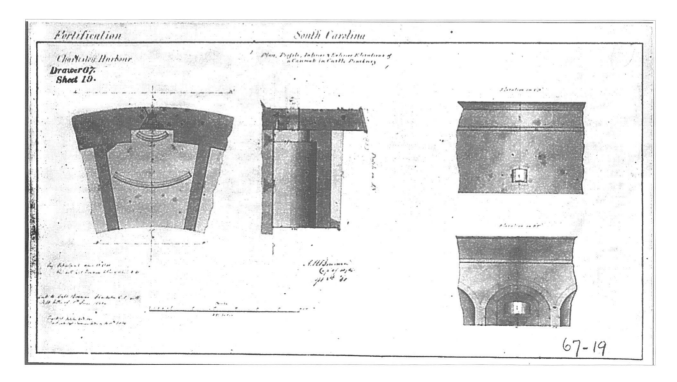

Top and bottom: Castle Pinckney profiles, sections, and elevations.

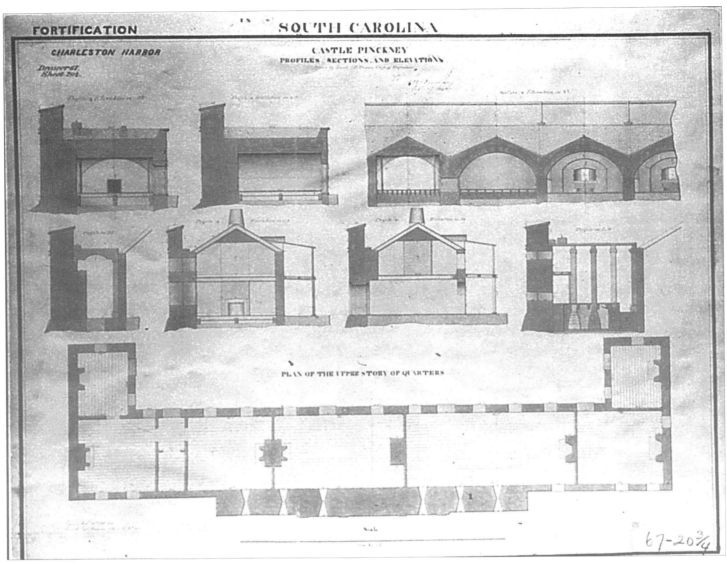

Castle Pinckney profiles, sections and elevations.

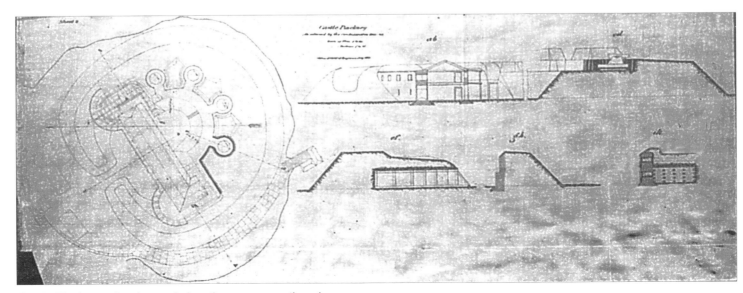

Castle Pinckney site plan and elevations as an earthwork.

The Ghosts of Castle Pinckney

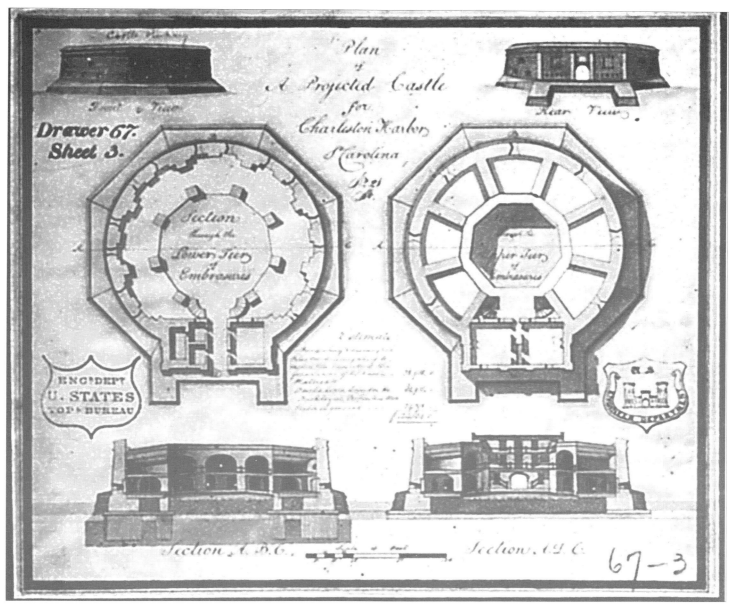

Proposed design for Castle Pinckney (never executed).

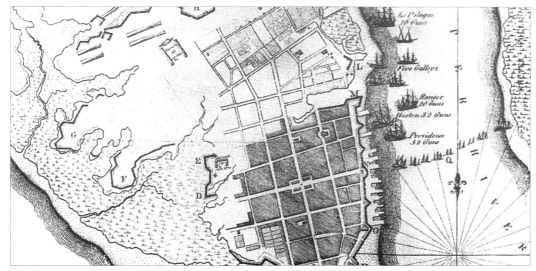

Note the line of sunken ships extending from Charleston across the Cooper River to Shutes Folly. Between five and fourteen vessels were sunk in an attempt to block the advance of British warships during the 1780 siege of the city.

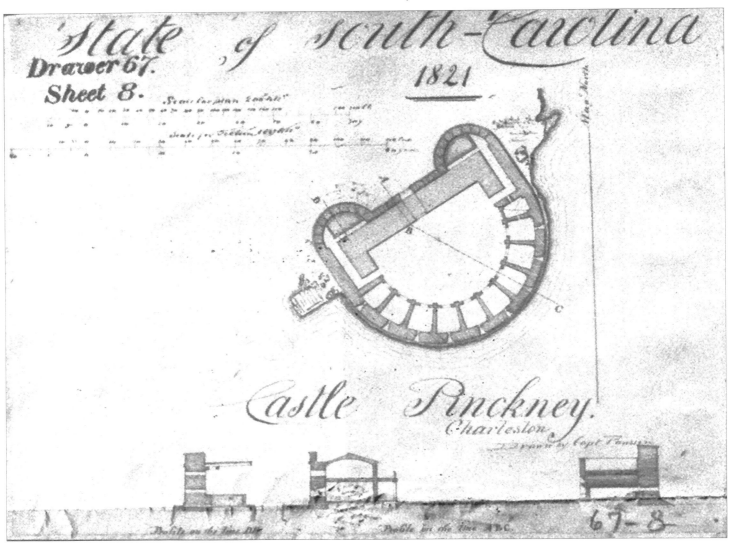

1821 drawing of Castle Pinckney by Captain Will Tell Poussin, topographical engineer.

1831 view of Charleston harbor, showing Castle Pinckney.

A Brief History of Castle Pinckney
Suzannah Smith Miles

It is the "other" island in Charleston harbor, the one closest to peninsula Charleston and easily seen from the Battery, often mistaken by visitors for Fort Sumter. Although not much remains of Castle Pinckney proper, and its thick brick walls are now crumbling amidst a tangle of wild vegetation, the site has a long and impressive history.

The actual name of this centrally located harbor island is "Shutes Folly." Like Folly Beach, the island, which was originally much larger, was named for the lush vegetation it once held – "folly" being an archaic term for a verdant thicket of trees and plants. The island's first historical mention is found in 1711 when its then-224 acres were deeded to Colonel Alexander Parris (for whom Parris Island near Beaufort was named), a commander of the South Carolina provincial militia.

By 1730, the island was under cultivation. In 1746, the island was deeded to a Quaker named Joseph Shute, thus the name "Shutes Folly." There is early mention of a grove of orange trees during the period of Shute's ownership and, indeed, during his time oranges were grown in Charleston and the surrounding areas in some abundance. The island remained in the Shute family until 1763.

The island's history during these early years is sketchy, at best. It may have been used by coastal Indians in some fashion, for old maps show circular formations of oyster shells which may have been shell middens. As early as 1717, there is mention that it was used as a place to hang convicted pirates; legend has it that their bodies were left hanging from the gallows as a deterrent to others who might consider entering into acts of piracy.

In 1805, fifty acres on the island were purchased by Jonathan Lucas, who, in 1795, had invented the first water-driven rice mill. Since maps of this period show a building on Lucas' property, it may be that he considered placing (or did place) a mill on the site.

Historically, the island's strategic harbor location gave it military significance but, in many ways, Castle Pinckney's military history is one that followed the adage, "always the bridesmaid, never the bride." The fort never quite attained full military importance. Even as early as 1736, when the first thought toward erecting a fortification on the island was considered, the intended fort was built instead at the point of Charleston's peninsula.

It wasn't until the American Revolution that the first fort was erected on the island and this was just a small earth-and-timber structure. In 1794, three years after his visit to Charleston, President George Washington ordered a fortification built on the island. In 1797, a fort of logs and sand, somewhat larger than the original, was begun. It was at this time that the fort was named to honor General Charles Cotesworth Pinckney of Revolutionary War fame. Facing southeast, this early fort was shaped in a half hexagon, mounted eight guns, and held quarters for a small contingency of officers and men.

The fort was destroyed by a hurricane in 1804. In 1808, it was entirely rebuilt, this time of brick, and constructed in a horseshoe shape. It mounted two tiers of cannon with a capability of holding twenty-one, possibly thirty, and had quarters for fifty men in peacetime and a hundred and five men when fully garrisoned. Despite the outbreak of the War of 1812 and Charleston's direct involvement in that conflict, the fort saw no action. By 1826, it was considered a "secondary" work by the defense department.

The island began to erode severely in the 1820s, causing further problems. In 1831, extensive repairs were necessary and stone embankments were put into place around the fort to fend off the encroaching sea. It was maintained by a small garrison and housed a post hospital. With the outbreak of the Second Seminole War in 1835, the garrison was moved to Florida and the fort was empty again.

It wasn't until the 1850s that Congress appropriated money to repair the fort and, in 1855, a navigation light was installed. Although the fort remained partially armed, it was ungarrisoned and was used primarily as a city powder storehouse. However, the fort was maintained by a retired federal ordnance sergeant and his daughter.

In December of 1860, with secession fever at its height, preparations were made to regarrison Castle Pinckney with U.S. troops. Seven days after South Carolina seceded from the Union, Lieutenant Richard Kidder Meade, an ordnance sergeant, four mechanics and thirty laborers were sent to clean up and repair the fort.

Following Major Robert Anderson's December 26th move of his garrison from Fort Moultrie to Fort Sumter (a step seen by South Carolina as a direct act of war), Castle Pinckney was taken without incident on the afternoon of December 27, 1860. A detachment from the 1st Regiment of Rifles, a militia under the command of Colonel John J. Pettigrew, landed on the island and knocked on the sally port door. Meade's men hid under beds and only the retired ordnance sergeant's daughter faced the militiamen, refusing them entry. The militiamen silently placed ladders against the walls and scaled them, retaking the fort. The militiamen took the island in the name of South Carolina, the only state which had, to this point, seceded from the Union. Lieutenant Meade later joined the Confederacy and served for the duration of the war.

Following the First Battle of Manassas (Bull Run) on July 21, 1861, Castle Pinckney was converted into a stockade for Union prisoners-of-war. It was garrisoned by the Charleston Zouave Cadets. One hundred thirty Union soldiers captured during that battle were held at the fort, including soldiers and officers from the 11th Zouaves, the 69th Irish Regiment, and the 79th Highlanders, all from New York, and the 8th Michigan Regiment.

After the prisoner exchange in October, the fort was converted back to a defensive work, although its location in the inner harbor made it less strategically important than other harbor fortifications. By 1864,

the fort's casemates were disarmed, the interior was filled with sand and, although four guns remained on the island, it saw no further action. On the night of February 17, 1865, the garrison raised its Confederate flag for the last time and evacuated under the cover of darkness.

Following the federal occupation of Charleston in February 1865, Castle Pinckney was again used for a brief time as a prison, primarily for captured blockade-runners and civilian prisoners. This was probably the darkest part of Castle Pinckney's history, for it was during this period that twenty-five soldiers who had participated in a mutiny were executed and buried on the island.

With peace, Castle Pinckney again fell into disuse. In 1878, with the island now under the control of the Treasury Department, the old walls were demolished and a lighthouse station and supply depot were built on the island, at which time a light-keeper's house and other buildings were erected.

In 1897, Abraham Charles Kaufman, a Charleston philanthropist, proposed using the island for a home for Yankee veterans of the Civil War. The sanitarium was to be named for Major Robert Anderson, the federal commander of Fort Sumter at the outbreak of the Civil War. Congress passed a bill appropriating money for the project, but nothing ever came of it.

The lighthouse station remained active until 1916, when it was abandoned. In 1917, the island was transferred to the U.S. Army Corps of Engineers, who used the island

buildings as a storage facility.

In 1924, Castle Pinckney was designated by President Calvin Coolidge as a National Monument and it seemed destined to be preserved as a historical site. By 1933, however, when it came into the hands of the National Park Service, it was not considered "significant" enough to merit this status and was declassified.

Castle Pinckney was at one time on the National Register of Historic Places. It was removed by the House Public Lands Committee August 15, 1951 and reverted to the U.S. Army Corps of Engineers.

In 1958, the island was sold to the South Carolina Ports Authority and, once again, plans were discussed towards erecting a museum on the site. Again, nothing ever materialized. The island remained unoccupied and its buildings empty. Finally, in December 1967, a tremendous fire broke out on the island, a blaze which destroyed the house and other wooden buildings on the island.

The island is now owned by the South Carolina Ports Authority.

There is hope that someday the site will be fully explored historically and archaeologically and that what remains of the original fort will be preserved. Let us hope that this work soon comes to pass, for Castle Pinckney holds an important place in Charleston's rich past. Until then, it remains an abandoned, silent sentinel in Charleston's harbor of history.

Return to Castle Pinckney

In October of 1996, the author returned to Castle Pinckney with his son Chris, Bill Smith (illustrator of the book) and Bill's wife Willette. The purpose of the trip was to allow Smith the opportunity to take these pictures and familiarize himself with the island so he could make the drawings.

Although none of the buildings were still standing, there were enough remnants of the foundations for Smith to get an idea of what it must have been like to live there.

The author pointed out locations where many of the stories took place – the slough, the creek, the cistern, the Dummy Line, the wall where he dropped the brick on the marsh hen, and much more.

The author found his visit a bitter-sweet experience, but his memories of the place are so endearing that they far overshadowed the sadness of seeing "his" island in ruins.